"You were angry with me for flirting with her, but it was all in the way of business, you know," he said, with a teasing smile.

"I was not angry because of that! I just felt ridiculous when you went hounding off to sit with her at dinner and foisted me on to Gordon in front of everyone. A lady has her pride, you must know."

He lifted a lazy eyebrow. "So has a gentleman, Miss Lyman. You might at least pretend a proper fit of pique."

"I think you mean jealousy, milord."

"If you insist on calling a spade a spade."

"I do, and I insist on calling embarrassment by its proper name, not jealousy."

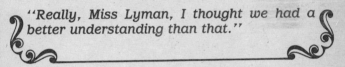

"Really, Miss Lyman, I thought we had a better understanding than that."

Also by Joan Smith
Published by Fawcett Books:

THE GREAT CHRISTMAS BALL

Joan Smith

FAWCETT CREST · NEW YORK

A Fawcett Crest Book
Published by Ballantine Books
Copyright © 1993 by Joan Smith

Library of Congress Catalog Card Number: 93-90526

ISBN 0-449-22146-6

Manufactured in the United States of America

First Edition: November 1993

Chapter One

Baron Costain sat at his desk in an austere office of the Horse Guards, gazing with unseeing eyes at the snowflakes that swirled beyond the window. On the scarred oak desk before him rested a booklet outlining procedures for handling such sensitive state secrets as came within his purlieu as assistant to Lord Cosgrave, who was in charge of espionage for His Majesty and the government of England.

Thus far, and he had been there a week, the only document entrusted to him was the outline of procedures. It was obvious Lord Cosgrave resented his appointment, and meant to keep him in the dark. The situation was intolerable! Lord Costain's bona fides were above reproach. He was the younger son of one of England's oldest noble houses. His father, the Duke of Halford, had served as an illustrious minister in two cabinets, and his older brother would follow in Papa's footsteps as soon as the Tories were put to rout. For centuries the Halfords had protected king and country.

Lord Costain's own career included two years fighting against the French in the Peninsula, before being sent home to recuperate from a ball taken in the left leg. What, exactly, were Lord Cosgrave's credentials other than his being a staunch Tory and friend of the Duke of York and the Prince Regent?

York and his cronies had badly mismanaged affairs in the Peninsula, sending Wellington out to battle the French with only a handful of foot soldiers and less than four hundred cavalry, forgetting transportation entirely. If Wellington had not gotten around them by picking horses up in Ireland, there would have been no transportation for supplies. The Joint Chiefs of Staff invariably demanded retreat when victory was in view and attack when defeat was inevitable. Well, all that had changed now, but at the Horse Guards, espionage was still in chaos.

Lord Castlereagh had dropped Costain the hint that someone was either being criminally careless or was a traitor. Important documents went missing, and subsequent events suggested they had reached Bonaparte's hands.

"I need a pair of sharp eyes to discover what is afoot," Castlereagh had said. "You will have to work under Cosgrave, unfortunately. To put you in over his head is as good as announcing your mission. But you will find a way. I have complete confidence in your abilities and discretion, Costain."

Lord Costain had exercised both faculties in the execution of his duties, but picking Cosgrave's lock and rummaging through his papers had thrown up nothing but a batch of billets-doux reeking with impropriety. Strangely, the female addressed her lover as "My dearest Cosgrave," but signed herself "Your faithful dove." And Cosgrave, fool that he was, kept the letters in his desk, where anyone might come across them and use them to pry war secrets from him. They would make juicy reading in one of the more scurrilous journals. What right had such a man to be in charge of espionage, if he could not even manage his amours with discretion?

Costain was interrupted by a knock at the door, and a senior clerk stepped in. "This just came in," he said, handing a note done up with sealing wax to Lord Costain. "Better get it to Lord Cosgrave as soon as he returns. He's at one of his meetings—they go on for hours. His secretary is not around, and Burack stepped upstairs for a word with Jenkins. I would not like to leave the note unattended."

A blaze of interest glowed in Lord Costain's dark eyes. "Where did it come from?" he asked.

The clerk said in a confidential voice, "A fellow who calls himself Mr. Jones. German accent. His letters are always treated with the greatest respect. He usually sends a messenger. That he risked coming in person suggests it is extremely important."

"Where is he?"

"When I told him Cosgrave was busy, he gave me the note and left. You'll handle it?"

The clerk's office was on the floor below. The mysterious Mr. Jones had had ample time to disappear. "Certainly," Costain said, looking at the note.

As soon as the clerk left, Lord Costain closed his office door, removed from his pocket a clasp knife, and heated its paper-thin blade over the flame of his lamp. He slid the blade under the sealing wax and removed the seal in one piece, to replace later by reheating. When he opened the sheet of paper, a frown settled on his face. "Damnation!" he muttered. It was written in German. After a career in the diplomatic service, Cosgrave spoke German. Lord Costain did not. Nor could he take it to their staff interpreter, as that would tell Cosgrave he had opened it.

He frowned over the unintelligible words but could make nothing of them. Whom could he trust to translate the thing, and do it in a hurry, before

3

anyone returned? His frown softened to interest, then escalated to a grin of nervous triumph. On his reconnaissance of the neighborhood, he had seen a small sign on a side door of a house on King Charles Street. MR. REYNOLDS, DISCREET TRANSLATION SERVICES PERFORMED. FRENCH, ITALIAN, SPANISH, GERMAN, RUSSIAN.

Thinking that such a service might come in handy one day, he had made inquiries for this Mr. Reynolds and discovered him to be a gentleman retired from the diplomatic service. He was trustworthy, elderly, and did not mix much in society. By God, he'd do. Cosgrave was at what the Horse Guards chose to call a meeting, which might last for several bottles. Costain stuck the letter in his inner pocket, put the button of ceiling wax in behind it, and peered out the door. He must have the letter back before Cosgrave returned, in case the clerk told him of its arrival.

It would be very interesting if Cosgrave gave Castlereagh some different interpretation of the note than he got from Reynolds. Castlereagh had told him to check up on everyone, and in Costain's mind, everyone included even the head of security. He did not actually think Cosgrave was a traitor, but it was possible his German was faulty. Improper translations seemed exactly the sort of foolishness to be expected from York's set.

He put on his coat, curled beaver, and York tan gloves, picked up his malacca cane, and stepped out the door. No one observed his departure as he stepped quickly along the corridor and out into the swirling snow. His leg ached a little in this raw, wet weather, but he was happy to see he had no need of his cane. He would soon be able to return to the Peninsula. He hastened through the storm toward the house on King Charles Street.

Snowflakes whirled in the darkening air of December beyond the window of the house on King

Charles Street. Cathy Lyman glanced up from her novel and gazed idly at the snow. It reminded her that Christmas was fast approaching, and the Great Winter Ball, that was to be *the* social event of the Season. Not that Christmas would be celebrated with any lavish festivities as it had been when Papa was alive, and not that she would be attending the ball. Mama had announced that morning that the tickets were an exorbitant price, twenty-five pounds a couple. Even if it was for charity, Lady Lyman could not see her way clear to laying out fifty pounds for a ball when the roof needed new slate. With Gordon at home, he would want to attend, too, and of course they could not offend Rodney by not inviting him.

Cathy drew a sigh and returned her attention to her book. The weather jarred sadly with the mood of the novel, *An Italian Romance*, by Mrs. Radcliffe. Cathy often read when she had no translations to do for her uncle Rodney. She found that Mrs. Radcliffe's gothic novels helped inject a little vicarious excitement into the tedium of her life.

Mama had given her brother, Rodney Reynolds, the use of the west wing of the house when Papa died. The space consisted of the library and a study which Rodney used as his private office. Mama liked to have a man on the premises, and Rodney was no trouble to her at all. He was a sad trial to Cathy, as the library was her favorite room, but really he spent most of his time in his office.

Rodney's diplomatic career had not been so distinguished as Sir Aubrey Lyman's, of course. Papa had received a baronetcy for his invaluable service abroad, and the taming hand of time had not dimmed the tarnish of his reputation in this household. Sir Aubrey was spoken of with a devotion bordering on idolatry. Yet his invaluable service had not left them very well off.

They had the house, and Mama's dowry, and wonderful memories of a youth spent in the gilded capitals of Europe, meeting the great and near-great. Cathy regretted she had been so young at the time, and could not attend the brilliant balls and parties. She had been only fifteen when Papa retired, but she had at least *seen* Napoleon's first wife, Josephine, and Metternich, and that wily Frenchman, Talleyrand. Such heady stuff had spoiled her for the few modest gentlemen who offered for her during her Season. Her high hopes had deliquesced, over the years, to a sort of dissatisfied resignation to her lot. With a reserved disposition and a modest nature, she could not make the sort of push her small dowry required to nab a good parti, so for the present, she lived vicariously through Mrs. Radcliffe's beleaguered heroines.

Mama often regretted that their high friends had deserted them when Papa died, but she did not regret it enough to pursue her past acquaintances. She was happy to be settled in a house of her own at last, and did not much care if she ever left it again. She had her few close friends, and now followed the news of the world desultorily through the journals and such gossip as came her way, living largely in the past.

Although Cathy was nearing five and twenty, she was still too young to live entirely on her memories and Mrs. Radcliffe's fiction. She looked forward with eagerness to her brother Gordon's entry into the diplomatic service. He had promised she might be his hostess. They had already decided his first posting would be to Rome.

Gordon had recently been sent down from Oxford for some boyish shenanigans involving a donkey and a don's chamber. To Oxford's relief, he did not plan to return. He was studying languages under Rodney's tutelage instead, in preparation for their sojourn in Italy. Meanwhile, Cathy helped their uncle with his translating chores, hoping some romantical job would come along. Truth to tell, very few jobs of any sort fell to their lot. Her uncle's main work since retirement was the translation of a German philosopher called Schiller, whose writings sounded exceedingly dull to Cathy.

As the weather was so cold that afternoon, she had not even taken her usual walk, but had remained at home and done a small job for her uncle. A Mr. Steinem had brought a billet-doux in German to be put into proper English. It was a tawdry thing, merely an assignation to meet his beloved at the southwest corner of St. James's Park at midnight. Was the lady married? He had addressed her as his "Dearest Angelina," which told her nothing, but surely a maiden would not be so dashing.

Cathy was disturbed by a light tap at the door, and looked into her uncle's private office. Rodney had left. He often slipped up for a nap at the end of the afternoon. It would probably be Mr. Steinem, come for his letter. When she opened the door, a gust of cold air and even a few snowflakes blew in.

She saw a curled beaver bent against the wind, and a set of broad shoulders in a greatcoat. "You had best come in, Mr. Steinem," she said.

The hat lifted, and she found herself gazing at a face that bore no resemblance whatever to Mr. Steinem's sturdy Teutonic visage. The first thing she noticed were the eyes—dark, flashing eyes topped by slender arched eyebrows that lent the man's face an expression of surprise.

When he stepped into the room, she noticed his complexion was swarthy. He removed his hat, and she saw that his hair was jetty black, barbered in the stylish Brutus do. Italian? Spanish? French? The features were regular, the nose pronounced but refined, the jaw rugged.

"A nasty day," he said in the accent of an English gentleman. His smile was nervous, his whole body tense.

"Yes. I was expecting someone else," she explained with an answering smile.

Snow coated the shoulders of his coat in white

stars. "Perhaps you would like to remove your coat and shake off the snow," she suggested.

"I'm afraid I'm wetting your carpet," he said, sliding out of his coat to reveal an outfit of the first stare. A jacket that Gordon would immediately recognize as the work of Weston hugged a pair of broad shoulders. The waistcoat was gold, striped in thin lines of mulberry. The cravat was unexceptionable, the Hessians gleaming beneath a few drops of water. He shook the snow off his coat on the stone apron of the grate and set his coat aside with a graceful movement.

This gentleman was far from the usual sort of client. What could Mrs. Radcliffe not make of him! Cathy felt a ripple of interest. "What can I do for you, Mr.—?"

His hand shot out. "That's Lo—Lovell. Mr. Lovell." Best to keep his real identity concealed. "I would like to speak to Mr. Reynolds, ma'am."

Cathy felt her fingers being pressed in a firm grip. If he had thought of her as a young lady, he would have bowed. "Miss Lyman," she said. "Perhaps I can help you. I do some translating for my uncle. If your translation is Italian or Spanish, I must call my uncle. I do only French and German."

"Is he about?"

"This is his hour for a nap. If you are not in a hurry, I shall call him."

Lord Costain was in very much of a hurry. The lady was Reynolds's niece; she must be all right. He took his decision in a split second. "It is German, actually," he said, and removed the letter from his pocket. "Your sign says discreet translations. I trust I may rely on that? Actually the letter is not mine. A friend of mine has been abroad, and received this note. He did not know anyone who could translate it for him, and I had seen your sign outside."

"Do you live nearby, Mr. Lovell?" she asked, taking the note.

"No! No, I live on Upper Grosvenor Square," he said, hastily choosing an address far removed from his own Berkeley Square.

"Perhaps you work at Whitehall, as you have spotted my uncle's little sign?"

He read the intelligent interest in her look, and felt a qualm. "No, I happened to be strolling through St. James's Park one day, and wandered by your house in passing. My friend, the one who received the note, cannot imagine who could be writing to him in German. All a mistake, I daresay. Brown is a common name, after all." Now, why had he said that? Perhaps the letter used a different name.

A soppy love letter, Cathy said to herself, *and he is ashamed to admit it.* She was disappointed in him. Aloud she said, "It is not necessary to explain the note's history, Mr. Lovell. I merely translate. Will you wait? I see the letter is brief."

"Yes, certainly."

"If you would like to have a seat by the fire, I shan't be long."

"Thank you." He sat for a moment, but was soon up, pacing the room in obvious agitation.

Cathy drew out a sheet of paper for her translation and read the letter. A frown drew her brows together. This was no love letter! It spoke of *the gentleman's* defeat at Moscow, and plans by the German states to rise up against *the gentleman* while he was in disarray. *The gentleman* was obviously Napoleon Bonaparte, who had invaded Russia, and if Mr. Lovell was not a spy, she would be much surprised.

Her excitement rose higher as she realized what she was reading. The only question was, what sort of spy was Mr. Lovell? He had a Latin look about him, yet his accent was English. His tailoring did not suggest that he lived on Upper Grosvenor Square, and the fact that he knew of her uncle's

9

small translating service suggested that he did indeed work at Whitehall.

She peered over her shoulder, and saw him gazing at her in fixed concentration. She damped down her excitement and wild imaginings and translated the note. When she was finished, she said, "It is ready, Mr. Lovell" in a remarkably calm voice, but her hand was trembling.

He came pouncing forward at once. "How much—"

She leveled a penetrating look at him. "It was an honor to translate this one. You may tell Mr. Brown there will be no charge."

Their eyes met and held. He read the knowledge in hers, and his heart shriveled. "You know!" he said in a hollow voice.

"Yes, I know," she replied calmly.

His lips clenched in indecision, then he hastily read the note. When he was done, he lowered it and stared at Cathy. What must this prim little spinster make of all this? He was on thorns to dash to Castlereagh with the news. Castlereagh would be eager to abet Metternich and the Prussians to break the alliance with Boney. But he must get the letter back before Cosgrave discovered its absence. Most of all, he must secure this girl's promise to hold the secret.

"You realize this is strictly confidential, Miss Lyman."

"Of course," she said.

"I cannot overemphasize the importance of secrecy."

"My family have a long history in the diplomatic service, Mr. Lovell. Our word is our bond."

"You must not tell anyone, even your family."

"I understand. There is only one thing that bothers me. Why did you not use the translation service of the government? Why bring such a sensitive document to me?"

"Because there are people at work who are not

to be trusted. We do not know who is responsible, but secret information is leaving the Horse Guards."

She considered this a moment and found it reasonable. "I will be happy to perform any such work in future, without charge, naturally."

"And you won't tell anyone I was here. I have bent the rules a little. It would not be well for me if it were discovered."

"Yes, it was rather rash of you, Mr. Lovell," she said, but in no condemning way. "But you may place complete faith in my discretion."

Lord! He had placed state secrets in the hands of a mere lady. Even Castlereagh would not countenance this folly. He studied her a moment. Excitement lent a sparkle to a pair of hazel eyes heavily fringed in lashes. For the rest, she was rather pretty in a conventional way, with a tumble of brown curls and regular features. It was her prim manner that had suggested the word *spinster*, for she was certainly not old. None of this gave any indication of her character, however.

She mentioned her family's history. Lyman— what did he know of them? There was a Sir Aubrey Lyman. "Are you Sir Aubrey's daughter?" he asked.

"Yes," she said proudly.

"Ah, and where is he posted now?"

"He has been dead these five years."

"I'm sorry," he said perfunctorily. His overriding concern was to discover something of the family's character and reputation, but he had not time to do it then. "My family was acquainted with him some years ago," he lied smoothly. "Could I do myself the honor of calling one day?"

"We should be happy to receive you." She smiled.

Her shy smile told him she had taken the gesture as a personal compliment. Was there no end to the mischief he could create? "Will you be at home this evening?" he asked.

"Oh, yes, we seldom go out. In such weather as this, I mean," she added hastily, as she did not wish to give Mr. Lovell the notion she had no social life.

"It begins to look as though we shall have a white Christmas." He smiled, putting on his coat. "I don't know how to thank you, Miss Lyman." He picked up his hat and cane.

"You will remember to return if you have any other documents to translate."

"Indeed I shall."

He tipped his hat, opened the door, said *"Au revoir,"* then disappeared into the darkness, cursing himself for his incautious behavior. She was certainly eager to get her eyes on more state secrets! Surely the Lymans were not in league with the Frenchies. He seemed to remember Sir Aubrey had been stationed in France some years before. Diplomats had been known to turn their coats. Their having set up shop so close to Whitehall looked suspicious. No very grand shop either; there was no money to spare there. He would make inquiries and see what he could discover.

In the study, Cathy Lyman hugged her excitement to herself, and felt exactly as if she had fallen into one of Mrs. Radcliffe's novels. All that was lacking was the grove of ancient oaks and a gothic castle, but the hero more than compensated for their lack. She wondered how she would ever keep such a wonderful secret from Gordon. How he would love to be a part of it!

Chapter Two

Lord Costain returned to the Horse Guards with ample time to return the note to its original form. Fortunately, neither Cosgrave's secretary nor the junior assistant, Mr. Burack, was about. He reheated his thin blade and returned the button of sealing wax in such a way that his practiced eye could see no irregularity in its placement. He disliked to give such an important message to a man who had spent the past two hours imbibing wine. When Cosgrave had still not returned to his office at five-thirty, Costain took the letter to Lord Castlereagh, as it was too urgent to wait longer. He admitted frankly what he had done.

Lord Castlereagh, the foreign secretary, was a clever, dapper, rather handsome gentleman. He listened intently before speaking. "Rodney Reynolds, you say? He is sound as a rock, lad. No danger there. I have used him myself for personal matters."

"But it was his niece, Miss Lyman, who translated the note."

"Miss Lyman? Oh, dear, that was a tad rash. The young ladies are notorious for their flying tongues.

13

But then, Miss Lyman is no longer on the town. One seldom sees her out. And she has experience of sensitive matters—she was abroad for years with her father. Impress upon her that secrecy is of paramount importance."

"I did that, of course."

"Just one word of caution—she has a foolish, headstrong young brother. We don't want him working mischief on our behalf. You might call on her and tell her not to mention it to him. I shan't presume to tell you how to convince a lady," he said with a twinkle. "And now I must show this to Liverpool. One trembles to think we might not have seen it till morning if you had not chanced to be there. This is the sort of thing we have to put up with from York's set."

"Could Mr. Jones and all the Mr. Joneses not be instructed to deliver their notes directly to you, sir?" Costain suggested.

"It is not feasible to have them dropping into the House of Parliament. The function of the Horse Guards is to handle such matters, and sift the wheat from the chaff, for we get mainly chaff, you must know. Folks with a hankering for excitement and overly active imaginations see a French plot on every street corner. Cosgrave will soon be retiring. When we have the proper man in charge . . ." He gave a *tsk* of dismay. "Well done, Costain. I knew we might count on you. Carry on." He slid the note into his inner pocket and went off in search of the prime minister.

It was five o'clock. Cathy was eager to close the office for the day and have her tea. If Mr. Steinem did not come soon, she would do so. Meanwhile, she had plenty to fill her mind. The Great Winter Ball took a backseat to Mr. Lovell and espionage in her ruminations. Eventually, an image of her mama intruded. How could she explain Mr. Lovell's pending visit? He said their families were acquainted, but the only Lovell she could remember was a milliner, and Mama did not even like her bonnets.

The door from the hallway opened and a sleek head peered in. "Tea's on," Gordon said. "Cook has made hot scones. There's raspberry jam."

"I am waiting for a customer to return," Cathy replied.

A tall, elegant, slender form followed the sleek head into the room. At nineteen, Sir Gordon had acquired the height but not the bulk of manhood. His features were similar to Cathy's, with the same chestnut hair and hazel eyes, but with a stronger nose and jaw. As the sole son and heir of an illustrious father, handsome, not entirely stupid, and the apple of his mama's eye, Gordon felt he honored the world by condescending to decorate it with his presence.

He had left for university an unlicked cub, and come home a man of the world, but just what world his mind inhabited was unclear at present. He had arrived wearing the Belcher kerchief and wild hair of a poet, but when he had settled on a diplomatic career, he had switched to a proper cravat, got his hair barbered, and begun speaking in the oracular tones of his late papa when he remembered to. When he was hungry, as he was at that moment, he reverted to his own age and nature.

"Dash it, it's five o'clock. How long are you going to wait? It is unfitting for a Lyman to be taking in work from commoners."

"It is an affair of the heart," she replied with a forgiving smile. Gordon was suffering from his unrequited love for Miss Elizabeth Stanfield, and might accept this excuse.

"A lover should be more eager. To hell with him, say I. The scones will be cold."

"You go ahead." She was interrupted by a knock at the door. "Oh, here he is now."

She hopped up with alacrity to open the door and found herself staring at a curled beaver pulled low

15

and a scarf drawn high over a man's nose and mouth. All that was visible of his face was a pair of narrowed eyes, but she knew at a glance that the man was not Mr. Steinem. He was the wrong size, the wrong shape. He peered over her shoulder into the study at Gordon.

Before she could speak, the man jostled her rudely aside and stepped in. As she closed the door, a frisson ran up her spine. It was not quite fear; she was too annoyed to be afraid yet. It was not until she turned around and saw the black circle of a pistol barrel pointing at her that fear rose to engulf her. She looked in wordless horror to her brother, who gazed at the pistol as if it were Beelzebub incarnate.

"Give me the letter Costain left with you," the man said in a gruff voice. Cathy had the feeling he was changing his voice on purpose, making it a growl to frighten her.

"I don't know what you're talking about," she said in a trembling whisper.

"The man who just left—the message from Austria," he said impatiently. The gun moved in his hand.

Cathy felt ready to swoon. She had anticipated future excitement, but not of quite this sort, and not so quickly. At no time had a gun figured in it. Then she remembered Mr. Lovell. This was her chance to prove to him—why did this man call him Costain?—that she was fit to assist him. The intruder glanced at the letter on her desk, and she suddenly had the solution to her problem.

She picked up Mr. Steinem's billet-doux and her translation. The man grabbed them from her fingers and glanced at the original, then at the translation. "This is a love letter!" he exclaimed.

"That is what Costain left," she said with wide-eyed innocence. "You see the original is in German."

Gordon listened, and as the first terror subsided,

16

his mind began to work. It was clear to the meanest intelligence the man with the gun wasn't an outraged husband as he had first thought, or he would have been *expecting* a love letter. The only other possibility was that he was a spy. "It must be in code," he said without thinking. As soon as the words left his lips, he regretted it.

The intruder looked at him with interest, and seemed to accept the idea. He stuffed the letters into his pocket while still leveling the pistol at them with his other hand. "You two, down on the floor," he commanded.

"My good man!" Gordon said, bridling up.

"Do it, Gordie," Cathy said, and sat on the floor.

"Lie down, face to the floor, toe to toe," the man ordered. They did as he said. "You," he said to Gordon, "take off your cravat and bind your ankles together."

Gordon sat up, staring fixedly at the gun, undid his cravat, and did as commanded, but he tied the knot loosely. "Now lie back down," the man said. When they were flat on the floor, he put his gun aside a moment, but within his own reach. "Don't try anything," he cautioned in a menacing voice. He removed his gloves and tightened the knot. Gordon hadn't time, or perhaps courage, to try anything. The man picked up his gun and fled out the door.

As soon as he was gone, they both sat up and began struggling with the knotted cravat. "By Jove, a spy!" Gordon croaked, delighted now that the immediate danger was past. "I shouldn't have let out about the code. Fancy the mawworm not knowing it." When the knot proved incalcitrant, he took out his hasp knife and sacrificed his cravat.

As soon as he was free, he darted to the door, but of course the man was long gone. "His footprints are in the snow. I'll follow him," he said, and darted out into the evening shadows while Cathy sat gasping, wondering what she should do. She soon knew her first duty was to inform Mr. Lovell.

Within minutes Gordon was back, his head and shoulders lightly dusted in snow. "I lost him at the corner. There were a million fresh footprints. You would think an army had passed by. There wasn't a sniff of him."

"He probably had a carriage waiting," Cathy said.

"Damme! My first chance for a little excitement, and I not only let the bleater get away, I told him about the code."

Cathy did battle with her conscience, and decided that sharing Mr. Lovell's secret with her brother was the lesser of two evils, because Lovell must be informed at once, and she could not quite see herself going alone to Whitehall in search of him. She would tell Gordon the very minimum, just enough to ensure his help.

"That wasn't the letter he was after, Gordie," she said.

"Eh? What the deuce are you talking about? It was in German."

"That was Mr. Steinem's billet-doux. The man with the gun was after a different letter."

"The devil you say! What letter?"

"He took it away with him, the man who asked me to translate it. That intruder must have followed Mr. Lovell here, for Lovell was not gone above five minutes when he landed in."

"And who, pray, is Mr. Lovell?"

Gordon listened, entranced, while Cathy briefly outlined the visit.

"Wouldn't you know I would miss it!" he said when she was finished. "While I was wasting my time on irregular verbs, we had a spy calling. Thank God for that billet-doux! At least I need not feel like a traitor. But do you mean to sit there and tell me you have been translating state secrets? I don't believe a word of it. You've been reading Mrs.

18

Radcliffe again." His eyes traveled to the sofa by the grate, where the novel lay, facedown.

"You must help me, Gordie," she said with such a sober mien that Gordon believed her. Besides, she hadn't enough imagination to come up with a story like this. "I must inform Mr. Lovell of that man's visit. Lovell does not realize he is being followed. He might be killed."

"Where can I get hold of this Lovell?" Gordon asked.

"At Whitehall. He works for the Horse Guards."

"He *is* a spy, then! Why, that's just around the corner. I can be there in two seconds."

"Yes, we must go. I wish I had gotten a better look at the man. His shoulders were hunched up, but he was tall, I think. He was so muffled up, I saw nothing of his face except his eyes. They were close-set, and squinty."

"Nothing of the sort. He was a short fellow. His eyes were not really close-set. It was only his squinting that made them look that way. I noticed particularly. I caught a glance at his hands when he was tightening my cravat as well. I'd recognize those ugly digits anywhere."

"Was he wearing a ring?"

"No, but he had those short, flat fingers like Cousin Marion—as if he had ten thumbs."

"Oh." That did not sound like much of a clue to identification. "Perhaps Mr. Lovell will know who he is. We must go at once."

"You cannot think I will allow a lady to accompany me on such an errand!" he exclaimed, reverting to his father's manner.

Allow her! She was the one who translated the letter. But emotion was not her way, and she said calmly, "You would not recognize Mr. Lovell."

"They will steer me to him fast enough at Whitehall."

"There is some little doubt that Lovell is his real name. The man with the gun called him Costain. I

19

must go to identify him, for the letter was of strategic importance."

"Really!" Gordon exclaimed. "What did it say?"

"I promised Mr. Lovell I would not tell a single soul."

"Damme, you may tell me. I am no one—I mean, I am your brother."

"I cannot tell even you, but it is of such vital importance that it may alter the course of the war, Gordon."

Gordon gave a frowning "Hmmm," but he was actually less interested in the details of the war than in having a bit of excitement. "Let us go, then, if you insist on tagging along," he said.

"Yes—but what shall we tell Mama?"

"Why, we shall tell her we are working for king and country. She can hardly say no."

"She will say no to me," Cathy replied with irrefutable logic. "And besides, I was not supposed to tell anyone about the letter. I told you only because I need your help. You tell Mama I am waiting for Mr. Steinem, and will take my tea here in the office. You will have to sneak my bonnet and pelisse down to me."

"I shall tell her I am bearing you company. She has Rodney with her to prose her ear off, so she shan't mind. Best lock that door," he said, and left.

Cathy hopped up and locked the door, then drew the blue velvet curtains to ensure privacy from prying eyes. She felt a thrill, to think that someone might be peeking in the windows. She hoped Mr. Steinem would not come, for she had lost both his original letter and her translation. She wrote out a rough translation as well as she could remember, to stick on the door when she left. Mr. Steinem could pick it up, free of charge.

The tea tray arrived, followed a moment later by Gordon, bearing her bonnet and pelisse. She dressed, and they went out, leaving Mr. Steinem's note stuck to the door with a pin.

"I might very well be made a lord for this," Gordon said as they pelted through the snow. They did not wait for a carriage, as the distance was short. "I daresay Miss Stanfield would not wipe her feet on a mere baronet."

Gordon had his boots to keep his feet dry, but before they had gone a hundred yards, water was seeping through Cathy's slippers and freezing her toes. The wind blew her hair and bonnet to pieces, and found its way under her pelisse. She was hardly aware of the discomfort. In minutes she would see Mr. Lovell again, and she would gladly walk through fire or ice for his approval.

The yellow brick of Whitehall looked dingy in the fading light, but the many lighted windows gave them hope that Mr. Lovell was still there. The clock tower of the Horse Guards soon loomed ahead of them. They entered unchallenged, although a few eyebrows rose to see a young lady breach this masculine preserve.

"I am looking for a Mr. Lovell," Gordon said in a businesslike way to the guard.

The guard scanned his list. "No Mr. Lovell here, sir. Would it be the Admiralty you want?"

"Is there a Mr. Costain?" Cathy asked.

"Lord Costain, you mean, Lord Cosgrave's new boy? He's here. Went dashing out a short while ago, but he was soon back. Second floor, third door on your left."

"That'd be him," Gordon said. "Thank you, my good man."

As soon as they had gone beyond earshot, he said, "Dashed out and back again—bound to be our man."

Cathy had harkened to a different matter. "He called him *Lord* Costain!"

"No matter. It must be him."

"Oh, yes, I am sure it is."

They mounted the stairs, turned left, and counted three doors. The third door was ajar; a line of light issued from beneath it. Their pace increased as they drew nearer. Cathy felt nervous but excited.

Then Gordon turned to her and said, "What if it ain't him?"

"What do you mean?"

"What if the fellow who brought you the letter was a foreign agent posing as Costain, and you handed him over a translation of sensitive information? Are you willing to confess it, and be landed in the Tower?"

"It's got to be him," she said with more hope than certainty.

"Let me handle it. If it ain't him, we'll say it's a case of mistaken identity, we're looking for *Mr.* Costain. We'll dart home and ask Uncle Rodney's opinion. He'll know what to do. Put us on to someone important who won't throw us in the Tower when we confess what you've done. A bit rash of you, m'dear. You ought to have called me in sooner."

Cathy's heart was in her throat as Gordon tapped lightly on the door.

Chapter Three

"Come in," an authoritative voice called. *His* voice.

Cathy's smile told Gordon all was well. He pushed the door open and ushered her in. "I am Sir Gordon Lyman," he said, stepping forward and performing a ceremonial bow. "Have I the honor of addressing Lord Costain?"

Costain's eyes flew over his shoulder to Cathy. She read in them a mixture of astonishment, anger, and accusation. Before he could speak, she flew forward.

"The worst thing has happened, Mr. Lovell! Er, Lord Costain."

"How did you discover my name?"

"The guard downstairs told us there was no Mr. Lovell, but there was a Lord Costain."

"You must do better than that, Miss Lyman," he said, closing the door and staring at her in a vaguely threatening way. "It is unlikely the guard would leap from Mr. Lovell to Lord Costain with no additional clues."

"It was the man with the gun who called you Costain," she said.

"Gun? What man?" he demanded.

"The man who came to my office and demanded the letter you had brought me for translation. He must have thought it was a longer letter, that would require considerable time. That I still had it, I mean."

"Good God! Are you all right? He didn't harm you?"

"I am fine," she said, pleased at his concern.

"I am most sincerely sorry to have involved you in this, Miss Lyman. The man—can you describe him?"

"Not very well, for he was all muffled up, but he was tall, with close-set eyes."

"Short, with ordinary eyes, only he was squinting," Gordon amended, "and he had stubby, spatulate fingers."

"He looked tall to me," Cathy insisted.

"That is because you're a squab," her brother informed her.

Costain looked from one to the other in forgivable confusion. "You had best have a seat," he said. His worst fear had come home to roost. The hotheaded young brother was now in on the secret.

It was some quarter of an hour before the matter was fully revealed. "And that is why I had to tell Gordon, for I wanted to let you know *at once* that you were being followed, and I could not come out alone at night," Cathy concluded.

Costain paced to and fro, with one hand shading his brow to aid concentration. "Who could this man be?" Their description added nothing but confusion to the matter. He was tall and short, with close-set, squinty, ordinary eyes and short fingers. "He must have followed me from this building. I wonder if Cosgrave is having me followed."

"Lord Cosgrave?" Gordon asked. His questioning face told his opinion of this.

"Yes, he is my immediate superior."

24

Gordon rose at once. "I see. Well, we'd best be running along, then. All set, Cathy?"

Costain knew he had lost the young man's trust. Common sense told him the youngster's next move would be to inform Cosgrave of the whole business. He set himself to the task of charming them, and when Lord Costain decided to charm, he could bring the birds from the trees.

"You must allow me a few minutes to enlarge on the situation," he said. "Now that I have found such willing and able cohorts, I see I must tell you everything—on the understanding that it is strictly classified information. A glass of sherry, perhaps? His Grace sent me a few cases from Northland Abbey. You are perhaps familiar with the Duke of Halford, my father?"

As he spoke, he went to a cupboard and brought out a silver tray holding crystal glasses and sherry. Gordon hesitated. The words *willing and able cohorts* and *classified information* reeled in his head. Cathy gave a mental goggle at the casual mention of the duke, and fabled Northland, one of the finest estates in Kent. Even Mama would not object when she learned Mr. Lovell was the son of a duke.

"Perhaps a quick glass," Gordon said, and resumed his seat. "We missed out on our tea. Not that I am complaining! Though there were hot scones and raspberry jam."

"I used to like tea, but I gained a taste for sherry when I was in the Peninsula," Costain said. He meant to throw in everything that might impress the young fellow.

"You were in the Peninsula?" Gordon asked.

Cathy was a little disappointed in her hero. He was beginning to sound like a common, garden-variety braggart.

"The third son of the Halfords traditionally joins the army. I was sent home with a ball in the leg. Badajos," he said modestly.

"By Jove! What can we do to help you, Lord Costain?"

Costain trod a narrow path. It took him another quarter of an hour to convince the youngsters that they must not say a word to anyone, without giving them the notion Cosgrave was a traitor. He could not quite trust Gordon to act with propriety. He stressed the importance of secrecy, and of consulting with himself before doing anything.

"The very walls have ears," he said, glancing at the closed door. "It will not be safe for us to meet here. I shall call on you to arrange such matters as require your assistance."

"P'raps I could go with you tonight," Gordon said.

Costain blinked in confusion. "Go where?"

"Why, to the assignation. The letter Cathy gave the intruder set up a rendezvous at the southwest corner of St. James's Park at midnight. Since he thinks it is a code or some such thing, it stands to reason he will be there, don't it?"

"But if it is a code, then St. James's Park does not mean St. James's Park, and midnight does not mean midnight."

"Yes, well, he'll soon figure out it ain't *exactly* a code, and think it is a secret meeting instead. He will be there, depend upon it."

"You just might be right," Costain said with a tinge of respect. "But I shall not require your assistance tonight, Sir Gordon."

"What is my job tonight?" Gordon asked eagerly.

"It would be best if you circulate through the drawing rooms of London as broadly as possible, and see if you can recognize your intruder. One never knows, you might recognize him by the eyes, or the, er—thumbs."

"But I can do that anytime."

"The sooner you get a start on it, the better."

"Yes, but in this howling storm, the attendance at parties will be limited."

"It takes more than a snowstorm to slow the

26

Frenchies. Are we English to trail them in the pursuit of duty?"

"No, by gad. I shall go out if I have to take a shovel with me to clear my way."

Miss Lyman, Costain observed, was looking at him askance. She also had to be conciliated. "I trust you have not forgotten I am to call on you this evening, ma'am?"

"No, I have not forgotten."

"Will nine o'clock be convenient? I promise I shan't stay long."

"Stay as long as you like, Lord Costain," Gordon said. "I shall run along to my club for dinner, and see if I recognize the intruder."

Gordon was loathe to leave the office, but there were matters to attend to. He had to make some excuse to Mama for going out to dinner on such a night, and he wished to rag his valet into trying that dandy cravat knot Lord Costain was wearing. He set down his glass and rose. "Well, are you all set, Cathy?"

"Yes." She joined him. "I look forward to seeing you this evening, milord."

Costain took her hand and smiled into her eyes. "The hours will go on crutches until we meet again."

They left. Little conversation was exchanged during the walk home. It was not the wind whipping their coats and whistling in their ears that inhibited talk. Each was wrapped up in private reveries.

Costain sunk into his chair and stared glumly at their empty glasses. What had he done? He had saddled himself with a pair of youngsters who might take into their heads to tell the world of their great spying career if he did not keep a tight rein on them.

Honesty required him to admit, however, that it was entirely his own fault. It was he who had catapulted them into danger, and it was he who must ensure their safety as well as their discretion. He allowed they had been helpful thus far. It was kind of Miss Lyman to let him know he had been followed. Who could it be? Burack, the quiet man who occupied the office next to his own, and made such a parade of performing his job with efficiency? Or was it Cosgrave's right-hand man, Harold Leonard, hired especially by Cosgrave for the job? Or was it a genuine French spy, as the Lymans thought? The French might have been following Jones, seen him come to the translation service, and kept an eye on anyone leaving immediately after. He would drop around at St. James's Park at midnight to see if anyone showed up, though he did not think it at all likely.

On King Charles Street, Lady Lyman was in a decided pelter. Her offsprings' absence had been discovered, and she was waiting for them in her comfortable chair by the grate when they returned. Her cap of gray lace jiggled with annoyance. The same emotion drew her full face into an expression of petulance.

"Darting out without telling me, with the wind howling and the snow coming down in buckets. You have totally destroyed those good slippers, Cathy, to say nothing of wasting a very good tea. What was so important it could not wait?"

"Told you," Gordon said. "An accident at the corner. A rig overturned. I cannot imagine you did not hear it. You must be deaf as a doornail, Mama. If that team ain't lamed, it is more than I know."

"I knew there would be an accident sooner or later," Lady Lyman said with satisfaction. "It is a shame the way drivers are allowed to career about the streets. You'd best run up and dress for dinner, the pair of you."

"I will be eating out tonight, Mama," Gordon said. "Met a school chum—he was looking at the accident, too. The whole world was there—the ghouls."

"We also met Lord Costain," Cathy said. "He asked if he might drop in this evening."

The word *Lord* had a benign effect on Lady Lyman's mood. "Ah! Now, who, exactly, is Lord Costain? The name is not familiar. An earl, or a marquess?" She looked to her son, assuming the acquaintance had been made through him.

"A baron. The Duke of Halford's third son. He was in the Peninsula."

"The Duke of Halford's son?" She nearly jumped from her chair in delight. "Why did you not say so? What time is he coming? Cathy, run up and have Margold do something with your hair. You look for the world as if you had been on a sailing ship. Gordon, I did not know you knew Lord Costain. How did you meet him?"

"Why, you may meet him anywhere."

"Yes, but where?"

Cathy escaped gratefully upstairs, and left Gordon to invent an answer. She selected her toilette with care. It was not for the family that she chose her most flattering gown of pomona green sarsenet with the ruched skirt and put on her small emerald necklace, usually worn only to balls. She knew perfectly well she had no hope of attaching such a dasher as Lord Costain. Indeed, she had decided not to fall in love with him. He was too boastful to please her, but he was a handsome, eligible parti, and she wished to make a good impression.

Margold, her dresser and her mama's, dried her curls and arranged them *en corbeille*, with a green ribbon to set off their chestnut gleam. She took up a fringed paisley shawl and went below.

"Very nice, dear," her mother said, running a practiced eye over her daughter's toilette. "Does she not look handsome, Rodney?"

Rodney lifted his white head from the latest journal and harrumphed what might have been agreement. What he was really interested in was his dinner. The aroma of mutton filled the house. Food and drink were the sole sensual pleasures left to him, and even a scholar needed some sensual stimulation. "Did Steinem pick up his letter?" he asked Cathy.

"Yes, Uncle." It had been removed from the door when she and Gordon returned. As there was a half crown on the doorstep, she assumed Mr. Steinem had left it in payment.

Debrett's Peerage occupied the place of honor at Lady Lyman's right hand during dinner. She consulted it to discover what she could of the Halfords. She was flattered that Lord Costain claimed an acquaintance with the family, and concluded that it was his mama who had given him the notion. She was a Lady Mary Spencer before marriage. Lady Lyman had made her bows with a Lady Margaret Spencer, who was likely her sister.

Before Lord Costain arrived at nine-thirty, Lady Lyman was deep into plans for a small rout to celebrate the Christmas season and entrap Lord Costain, and Miss Lyman was on nettles. Cathy's body tensed like a coil when the door knocker sounded. And when Lord Costain was shown in, she admitted once and for all that she had never seen anyone so handsome. She had not thought it possible he could look better than he had that afternoon in his office, but she realized she was mistaken. The charm of immaculate linen against his swarthy complexion, the flush of rose in his cheeks from the weather, and the excellent tailoring of his black suit raised him a notch higher.

He glided forward, directing one quick smile at her before making a graceful bow to Lady Lyman and her brother, Rodney Reynolds.

"Have a seat, Lord Costain," the mother said. "What a frightful night for you to come out. Not the weather you were used to in the Peninsula."

"But a welcome change. In Spain one misses the snow. It is letting up now. In fact, the moon has peeped out, suggesting the storm has passed."

Lady Lyman cared no more for the weather than she cared for geometry. "How is your dear mama?" she asked. As she spoke, her hand yanked the bell-pull to summon her butler, who was asked to bring tea at once, for Lord Costain was perishing with the cold.

The leaping flames in the grate were more likely to melt than freeze him, but he was happy to be accepted with no hard questions. He knew, of course, that it was his eligibility and Miss Lyman's single state that paved his way. Another fine line to be trod.

When Lady Lyman said she would just remove a little from the grate and have a word with Rodney, Costain read her like a book. She wished to allow him privacy with Miss Lyman. As this was necessary, however, he smiled and rose to assist her with her shawl.

When he sat down again, he sat in the chair next to Miss Lyman. She leaned forward and said conspiratorially, "Gordon is out on the town, as you suggested. Have you learned anything of the mysterious intruder?"

"Not yet, but I shall keep the midnight rendezvous. You haven't mentioned all this to anyone?"

"No indeed! You may count on my complete confidence."

"I knew I might," he said, feigning a glow of admiration. He had no wish to discuss his business with a lay person, and subtly switched to other matters.

"What do you do when you are not engaged in espionage, Miss Lyman?" he asked with a bantering smile.

"I help Uncle with some of the simpler translations, and make a fair copy of a book he is translating. I am studying Italian, for when Gordon is sent to Italy—after he joins the diplomatic service, I mean—I shall be his hostess."

31

"Ah, Sir Gordon plans a diplomatic career, does he?" God help England, he said to himself.

"Yes, like Papa."

"Surely the study of Italian does not occupy all your time? What I was actually inquiring for was your amusements."

"The usual things," she said vaguely. "Parties, you know, and the theater, novels, and poetry."

He recalled Castlereagh's comment that she lived in a retired way, and felt that a further query on her reading would be the better tack to take. "A devotee of Byron, I expect?" he asked.

"No, he is too full of alarums and excursions for my taste. I prefer Mrs. Radcliffe."

"I had not thought she took a backseat to anyone in the area of alarums and excursions!" he said, and laughed.

"Yes, but her incredible tales are at least—" She came to a frowning pause.

"Credible?" he suggested.

"Not precisely, but I can put myself in the heroine's place, for she is a girl, whereas Byron's heroes are too grandiose for me. They are more like you," she said, much struck with this comparison.

"Grandiose! There is a facer for me! Upon my word, you are hard on me, ma'am."

"Indeed, I did not mean to offend you, milord," Cathy said, blushing prettily. "I was referring to your having been to Spain, and your title."

Costain studied her a moment. "Surely that does not earn me the opprobrium of being grandiose. I think you are referring to my boasting of them this afternoon, Miss Lyman. It was ill done, but I was concerned about your brother. I wanted only to ensure his going along with me."

Cathy considered it a moment, and said, "Yes, he is young and foolish enough to be impressed by such things."

"Whereas you are much too ancient to be impressed by my grandiosity," he said with a teasing look. "I have not observed any silver threads in your Titian curls. At what age does a young lady rise above such folly?"

"I expect that depends on the lady."

"And on her background. I understand you have traveled abroad?"

"I was taken abroad when I was too young to appreciate it. Now that I am old enough, I—" She came to a halt, wondering how she had been drawn into this personal sort of conversation. "But we were speaking of more important matters. I want to assure you I will always be available for any job you have for me. Gordon and I have been talking— in private, of course. We think the likeliest place to see our intruder is at the Horse Guards, so we shall walk past it several times tomorrow. We shall not go in, as you do not think it wise, but as we live nearby, it will be unexceptional to walk past early in the morning, when the workers are arriving, and at noon hour, when they are leaving, and again at the day's end."

Costain saw the subject was not to be avoided so easily as he had hoped. He also saw that his helpers planned to pester the life out of him. "Perhaps it would be best if you went in the carriage. The intruder would certainly recognize you, even if you did not recognize him. He would be suspicious to see you loitering about. Just a quick dash past at the hours you mentioned will suffice."

He could see she was dissatisfied with this meager help, and tossed a crumb of consolation. "I shall keep you informed of any significant happenings, of course. I would not like to take up your entire day."

"Nothing is more important to me than helping you, Lord Costain. Pray do not feel it is an imposition."

"You are very kind."

He succeeded in detouring the conversation to books and plays, and in half an hour he rose to take his leave.

"Half an hour. A very proper visit," Lady Lyman decreed when he left. "When will he call again, Cathy?"

"Very soon, Mama."

"Will he be in London at Christmas? You recall the rout party we are planning." As it was being planned solely on Costain's behalf, she was, of course, eager to ensure his presence.

"I didn't ask him."

"Ninnyhammer! Ask next time he comes. I do not wish to have all the bother of a rout if he will be going home to Northland Abbey."

"You must not assume he is courting me, Mama," Cathy said earnestly.

"Not courting you, when he comes out on such a night as this and sits with his head beside yours for half an hour in close talk? My dear child, allow me to know something of the world. That lad will come up to scratch before the winter is half over. I must have a look at *Debrett's* and see what estate falls to the third son. A pity he could not be the eldest son—a marquess, but there is nothing wrong with a baron, after all."

Mama soon took *Debrett's* to the lamp for close perusal; Rodney retired to his study, and Cathy sat by the moldering grate, waiting for Gordon's return.

Chapter Four

Gordon returned at eleven o'clock, cold, cross, and by no means sure Lord Costain was as sharp as he had first believed. "We have to talk," he said aside to Cathy as he entered the saloon.

Then to his mama he gave a brief description of his outing. "Nobody was out this evening. You could shoot a cannon down Bond Street without hitting a soul. I am frozen to the marrow and shall go directly to bed. Good night all." His commanding eye suggested that Cathy should also excuse herself.

Within minutes they met in the hall abovestairs. "Did he come?" he asked. She needed no reminder of who "he" was.

"Yes, as he said he would."

"What did he say?"

"He wants us to take the carriage tomorrow when we spy at Whitehall, in case the intruder sees us."

The lure of further involvement cheered Gordon and raised Costain a notch above odium. "A good idea. I mean to run along to the park tonight, just in case," he said.

"He told you he would handle it."

"How would you feel if he turned up dead in a ditch?" Gordon asked with a menacing squint. "Of course I must go. I daresay Costain expects it, but does not like to put a layman in jeopardy. Professional ethics," he explained vaguely.

Cathy pictured Lord Costain, his handsome features frozen to immobility in a ditch, and said at once, "I shall go with you." She was still uncertain about falling in love with Costain, but his conversation that evening had tipped the balance in favor of it. He had not seemed the least boastful when Gordon was absent. Besides, the Russian princess Katherine Bagration had strongly advised her, when she was fourteen years old, that she should have her heart broken as soon as possible, as it would inure her to cupid's arrows in future. Lord Costain appeared eminently capable of breaking a lady's heart.

"This is man's work," Gordon informed her with a condescending look.

"We shall go out by the study door" was her reply. "Rodney is not in his office tonight. Will you take a pistol, Gordon?"

Gordon did not argue further. Although more or less a man, he was five years younger than Cathy and somewhat accustomed to doing as she said. "I don't have one. I keep mine at Manton's Shooting Gallery. I must bring it home now that I shall be needing it."

"Then we must take some other weapon. Take your malacca cane, and I shall take Uncle Rodney's old blackthorn."

"You'd best not wear your emeralds" was Gordon's only animadversion. "Meet you in the study at eleven-thirty."

"The park is only five minutes away."

"The early bird catches the worm. We shall be there early and hide behind the bushes."

"That's a good idea."

Cathy nipped into her room and removed not only

her necklace but also her gown. After her chilling earlier in the day, she wore a warm suit under her oldest pelisse, with sturdy walking shoes and a large woolen shawl for extra warmth. The shawl could also be used as a headdress, as it would offer concealment if necessary.

They met in the study at the appointed hour. Gordon had arrived first and lit a lamp. He cast one glance at his sister and said, "Thank God it is dark out. You look like a beggar. I am ashamed to be seen with you. Here." He handed her Rodney's blackthorn walking stick, they extinguished the lamp, and crept silently out the door.

"Do you have the key?" he asked before closing it.

"No."

"Then we shall leave it on the latch to slip in later. There is nothing worth stealing in the study."

They hastened through the newly fallen snow that whispered underfoot. The storm had passed, leaving a black velvet sky sprinkled with stars. A crisp, cold wind snatched at their garments. No one else was about on this cold December night, but there were a few foot tracks in the snow. The only sound was the wind soughing through the trees, and the sussuration of their own feet in the snow.

St. James's Park was a vast black menace of ninety acres stretching before them. Nude branches etched a pattern against the sky. The untrodden snowfall at the park's edge told them they were the first to arrive.

"We shouldn't leave footprints. It might put the spy off," Gordon said.

They walked west along Birdcage Walk and entered the park from the southern side, working their way back through the concealing trees toward the southwest corner. Mist rose from the lake within the park, lending a dank atmosphere. Gordon did not think the rendezvous would take place deep within the park, but at the very edge. With this in mind, they stationed themselves behind a thick growth of shrubbery near the corner and hunkered down to wait.

The sound of nocturnal animals rustled from time to time, causing a flutter of excitement. It seemed an age that they waited. Gordon complained variously that his fingers were frozen solid, his legs asleep, he was certainly catching his death of cold, and he had never enjoyed himself so much in his life. One lone man passed within their view on Birdcage Walk.

"That's Lord Eldon, ain't it?" Gordon whispered. "I'd know his old hide in a tanning factory." The man lurched past without stopping.

At ten to twelve by Gordon's turnip watch, they espied a man slip into the park in a stealthy manner and station himself behind a tree. Like them, he had taken a circuitous route to avoid leaving footprints at the crucial corner.

"It's Costain!" Cathy said excitedly. "He came early, like us. Should we let him know we are here?"

"Best not. We'll just lie low and keep an eye on things."

Before long, a carriage drew up at the curb and another man in evening clothes descended. He stopped, looked all about, then walked into the shadows, to be swallowed by the night.

"Is that our intruder?" Cathy whispered.

"Damned if I know. We'll wait and see who else comes."

The next arrival was a lady, who came in a fashionable black carriage. She was accompanied by a footman. She was tall, and draped in a concealing black habit. The man who had arrived after Costain darted out to meet her. The couple climbed into the lady's carriage, but the carriage did not leave immediately.

"I daresay the spy could be a lady," Cathy said, frowning.

"More likely that lady is a man," Gordon replied. "She was tall as a ladder. By the living jingo, she's a man in disguise. We'd best accost them."

"Or—perhaps follow them?" Cathy suggested.

"We don't have a carriage. Why the deuce don't Costain make his move?"

Even as they spoke, the carriage began to draw away. Gordon left his place of concealment and called, "Lord Costain! Are you going to sit there and do nothing while they escape?" The echo of his voice shattered the stillness of the night.

Lord Costain's answering voice was drawn thin with aggravation. "Sir Gordon?" he called.

"Of course it's me. Let us take after them."

Gordon headed in the direction of Costain's voice, with Cathy darting after him. The night had been a sorry letdown. She had expected some heroics from her hero. An attack, gunshots, an arrest, perhaps, would have been interesting.

"Costain?" Gordon called again, for he could not seem to find his mentor. A dozen trees loomed before him, any one of which might conceal Costain. Why did he not answer? He heard a rustle in the bushes ahead, then the sound of rapidly retreating footsteps. "By Jove, he's turned tail and run. Costain!" he called after the fleeting footsteps. "Well, if that don' beat the Dutch!" He took another step, stumbled, and fell on his face.

An inhuman sound rent the air. "Aaargh!"

"What is it, Gordie?" Cathy asked, rushing forward to help him up.

"A body! I'm lying on top of it."

He leapt up as if the body might be infected with the black plague. Peering down, he saw a dark head, with a curled beaver lying beside it. The body was covered in a dark cloak.

"We'd best have a look and see who it is," Gordon said in a hollow voice. He already had an idea who it was. That black head had a familiar shape. He leaned down and gently turned the body over.

Cathy saw a pale face wearing the features of Lord Costain. A trickle of black moved inexorably down the side of his forehead, into his hair. She had never swooned before in her life, but she swooned then, sagging against her brother. "You've killed him!" she gasped.

"I? No such a thing. I don't even have a gun."

She leaned down and touched his cheek. "He's cold," she said.

"Of course he's cold, lying on a bed of snow. Check his heart."

Her trembling fingers moved his cloak aside and slid under his jacket. She felt his body warmth emanating from the strong wall of his chest beneath her fingers. There was a faint heartbeat. She looked at his face, as still as death, and her heart stopped. "Get a doctor at once," she said.

Costain's eyelids fluttered open, and he gazed at her in confusion. "The left flank!" he said, distracted. "For God's sake, cover the left flank. There are hundreds of them."

Cathy jumped back. "He is delirious, Gordon."

"Thinks he is back in Spain, I daresay. At least he is alive. I say, Costain—"

Lord Costain looked up at the sky and frowned. What was that white stuff on the trees? Snow? Snow! "Good Lord," he said, and sat up, shaking his head. "Did you see him? Did you get a good look at him?"

"We saw him right enough," Gordon said. "Why did you not follow him? It is my thinking that the lady he met was a man in disguise."

"No, it was Angelina Mc—er, it was a lady right enough. The billet-doux was just a billet-doux after all, but your intruder mistook it for a code. I meant, did you see the fellow who cracked me on the skull."

"We never got a whiff of him," Gordon said. "He must have come in t'other way and slipped up behind you."

"Are you all right, Lord Costain?" Cathy asked.

40

He touched his head tenderly. "I shall be as soon as you two stop spinning in circles." Gordon helped him to rise, and steadied him on his feet.

"You must get that bruise looked at, Lord Costain," Cathy said.

He drew out a handkerchief and patted the blood away. "How do you two come to be here?" he asked, his manner stiffening. "I told you I would handle this. This is no place for a lady, Miss Lyman."

"I told her so, but you might as well talk to the hat stand," Gordon said. "Anyhow, it is well we came, or you might have lain in the cold all night and come down with pneumonia. Go on home, Cathy. I'll get Costain to a sawbones. Did you bring a carriage, milord?"

"No, I came in a hansom. I do not require an escort home," Costain assured his young rescuer. "I shall find a hackney cab. You take your sister home, Sir Gordon."

"We cannot let you wander the streets alone in your condition," Cathy said firmly. "We live around the corner. You must come home with us." She turned to Gordon. "We'll take him into the study. No one will know."

"A capital idea. A good thing I thought to leave the door on the latch."

Costain said, "Just accompany me until I find a cab. I shan't bother you further."

There was no cab to be found, however, and when they reached King Charles Street, Costain felt so faint that it seemed best to stop a moment. He was helped along with great solicitude, guided up the steps and onto a sofa before the cold grate. While Gordon built up the fire, Cathy poured him a glass of sherry.

"Ask Simmons for a bowl of water and a plaster, Gordon," Cathy said. "Tell him you cut your finger."

Gordon wrapped his handkerchief around his hand and went after Simmons for the necessary supplies. Gordon took the water and plaster to the study.

"I am sorry to be such a nuisance," Costain said two or three times, while Cathy attended to his wound. He was very pale.

"I hope I am not hurting you," she said, daubing tenderly at his cut.

He smiled wanly. "Our nurses at Belem, in the Peninsula, did not have such a gentle touch," he said.

As she worked over him, he noticed the sweep of dark lashes against her cheek. Then she glanced up, and he observed the concern in her youthful eyes. His look caused a flush to brighten her cheek. She moved to arrange his pillow, and he was struck by the litheness of her form. Something stirred in him. Miss Lyman's beauty was not of the sort that leapt out and assaulted a man at first view. It was a more quiet charm that showed best under duress. He suspected she was shy.

"You will be wishing me at Jericho," he said.

"I think the shoe is on the other foot, milord. It is our fault. If Gordon had not shouted your name, perhaps the man would not have discovered your presence."

"There is no saying. He did strike immediately after Gordon called, but he must have been creeping up on me before. I am a poor advertisement for a *guerrillero*. I was taught to be able to handle myself in such situations. I shall blame it on the snow. It muffled his footfalls." He winced as she bathed his wound.

"Sorry. You didn't catch a sight of him?"

"Not so much as a glimpse. He came from behind. Just as I heard him and turned, he struck me. I fancy he was only trying to get away unseen."

"Then he must have feared you would recognize him," she said.

"All I saw was a hand," Costain said.

"With stubby fingers?" she asked with a facetious smile.

Costain felt an answering smile creep across his lips. He enjoyed her fussing over him, which was strange, as he had particularly disliked such attentions at Belem. It was because she was a woman, of course. Really quite an attractive woman when she smiled. "Actually he wore a glove. It may have been a common thief—but no. A thief would not have struck when he knew I had help close by."

"Help, or hindrance?" she asked, shaking basilicum on the plaster.

"Let us say colleagues, to avoid calling a spade a spade."

"I wonder if a spade minds being called a spade. Is your money purse missing?"

He felt for it. "No. And my watch is still with me. I think we can assume your intruder went to the park in hope that the lovers' rendezvous was something else. A pity he saw me there."

She leaned over him and gently applied the plaster. "I hope that wound he inflicted is not too uncomfortable."

He lifted his hand to pat the bandage, and their fingers brushed. Cathy hastily withdrew hers. "You do it," he said, lowering his hands.

She pressed tenderly on the plaster. "Does that hurt?"

"A mere bagatelle to a veteran of Badajos, I promise you—that little bit of boasting is just for you. Don't tell Gordon. But I didn't mean this lump on the head when I said it was a pity he saw me, Miss Lyman. The fact that I was aware of the rendezvous tells him you are working with me. How else could I have known of it? I may have put you in danger," he said, and gazed at her a long moment. Cathy was beginning to feel the greater danger was in his eyes that held her mesmerized. "You did not catch sight of my attacker?" he asked.

"No, he must have been there before any of us."

Costain nodded. "Gordon will dislike it, but I think I really must ask you two to resign."

"You're right. We are more harm than help," she said reluctantly. "I shall miss the excitement."

"You are developing a taste for alarums and excursions, are you? Take care, or you will find yourself enjoying Byron."

"I shall place the blame in your dish, sir."

Gordon returned with the tea tray. "I have just had a capital notion, Costain," he said, smiling from ear to ear. "What you said about it looking suspicious, my hanging around the Horse Guards—"

"Yes, I do think it a poor idea," Costain said at once.

"So do I. The thing to do, I'll sign up to work for them on a full-time basis."

Cathy could almost hear Costain's inward groan. "They aren't hiring at the moment," he said quickly.

"That will be no problem. Mama knows everyone. You would never guess it, the way she hugs the grate, but she has connections throughout society. She will arrange it, never fear. Do you think I could get an office next to yours?"

"That office is taken. The Horse Guards has certain requirements for recruitment, Sir Gordon."

"Call me Gordie. All my friends do. As to requirements, dash it, I have two years at Oxford. I can parlay the old bongjaw as well as a Frenchie. Papa made a point of our learning languages. I can scribble up a pretty good fist. I shan't mind what job I am given—scribbling out letters, or what have you. Dash it, I'll even make the tea."

Cathy said, "This is nonsense, Gordie, and you know it. What do we know of spying? We are nothing but a nuisance to Lord Costain. I have just been telling him we shan't involve ourselves further in his business."

"Speak for yourself," Gordon said, unfazed. "I

shall drop around Whitehall tomorrow and see who I can pester into giving me a post."

Costain felt this was to be avoided at all cost, and said, "Do you know, Gordie, I think it would be better if you remain anonymous. You could be of more use to us in a free-lance capacity." He looked over Gordon's shoulder to Cathy, who shook her head in amusement.

Gordon looked interested. He did not really relish sitting behind a desk. *Free lance* had a dashing sound to it. "What did you have in mind, Costain?"

"It would be a great help to me if you could follow certain people," he said, rapidly inventing an imaginary chore to keep the boy busy.

"It will require a disguise, of course," Gordon said knowingly.

"Oh, certainly! A disguise is of the essence."

"Who is it I am to follow?"

"A fellow at the office." He stopped, ransacking his mind for some harmless person. "Mr. Leonard, Cosgrave's secretary," he said. "He lives on Half Moon Street." As Mr. Leonard would be in the office all day, Costain added, "And his wife. It would be helpful if you could discover something of her doings."

"A shady wife, eh? Sounds pretty suspicious to me."

Costain and Cathy exchanged a secret smile. Costain said, "Highly suspicious."

"Can you describe her?"

"No, you'll have to discover which house on Half Moon Street the Leonards live in. When you see a lady come out, don't let her out of your sight."

"I'll stick like lint on a coat sleeve. You can count on me."

"England counts on you."

"England couldn't be in better hands."

Gordon was in alt with his new assignment, and spent the next five minutes discussing his disguise. He would dress as a chaplain, in his late father's black coat and a rusty hat. When Lord Costain was sufficiently recovered to leave, Gordon darted out to see if he could find a hansom.

Cathy and Costain went to the door. "Well," she said quietly, "it seems this is good-bye, Lord Costain."

He lifted his finely arched brows in disagreement. "Coward! Would you abandon me to Gordie's machinations when it is you who brought him down on my head? I shall require a deal of assistance in devising jobs for him."

"I suspected Mrs. Leonard was a ruse."

"I shall call on my way to Lady Martin's rout tomorrow evening to get Gordon's report." He hesitated a moment, then said, "It is possible your intruder will be there, as Sir John Martin works at the Horse Guards. You might recognize him—there is no saying. Actually seeing him again might trigger a memory. I wonder—would your mama let you come with me?"

"Yes, she would," Cathy said with no coy demur.

"Shall we say nine o'clock?"

"That will be fine, milord," she said primly, damping down her delight.

"*A demain*, then." He bowed and left, just as Gordon hailed a hansom.

As Costain drove home, he wondered if he was being rash. Lady Lyman certainly had him in her eye as a prospective son-in-law. His intention was to return to Spain as soon as his job at the Horse Guards was done and the doctor considered his wound cured. It would be unconscionable to become involved with a lady when he had no intention of marrying her. Cathy Lyman, he thought, was not a lady who took her affairs lightly. There was nothing of the flirt or coquette in her. Then, too, she was no longer a deb. She would be interested in finding a match soon.

He would dilute that visit to Lady Martin's rout

by inviting Gordon as well, and making it very obviously a working engagement.

When she lay in bed that night, Cathy's thoughts did not turn to marriage. Costain had made it perfectly clear their evening out was strictly business. She felt Lord Costain was miles above her, and hoped only that Mama would not frighten him off. It would be amusing to go about to a few parties with a handsome parti, even if there was no romance in it. She might meet someone who could love her, and if she did not—well, it would pass the time until Gordon went to Italy at least.

Chapter Five

Well satisfied with her perusal of *Debrett*'s, Lady Lyman made a grande toilette to greet the third son of the Duke of Halford the next evening, and even condescended to loan Cathy her second-best string of diamonds for Lady Martin's rout. "For he has already seen your emeralds," she pointed out. "We would not want him to think you have only one decent necklace. It is not really deceitful, for I have decided to give you this necklace as a wedding gift, Cathy."

"It is only a rout party, Mama. You must not raise your hopes too high," Cathy said, but she was happy for the loan of the diamonds. They lent a note of elegance to an otherwise indifferent toilette. Her burgundy gown, while of the finest silk and in excellent condition, was three years old. Cathy had adopted the strategy of choosing plain designs that did not go out of style quickly. Embellished with a new shawl or ribbons or jewelry, they served through several changes of fashion.

"*Only* a rout, when he has invited Gordon to go with you? My dear, that betokens serious intentions. A gentleman does not invite his lady's brother along unless his intentions are honorable and serious."

"Your mama is right," Rodney said. "If he did not want to catch you, he would not be angling in this stream." He didn't believe a word of it, but he liked to agree with his sister when it did not impinge on his own comfort.

By the time Costain arrived that evening, Lady Lyman was in possession of the name of his estate. Her reading had informed her that Lord Costain was heir to Pargeter, in Wiltshire. To discover something of its extent, she said, "Will you be spending Christmas with your family, Lord Costain, or at your own place in Wiltshire?"

"If I leave town, I shall be going to my parents' home," he replied vaguely.

"And who looks after Pargeter for you during your absence? It is not wise to abandon an estate to servants for too long. They tend to let the place deteriorate. Is it cattle you raise at Pargeter?"

"Some cattle," he said, "but my bailiff is also my cousin, who takes a keen interest in the estate. I daresay he runs it better than I could myself."

"A large place, is it?"

"It was originally small, but over the years—before my time—it has grown to a thousand acres, I believe."

"Ah." She nodded. "And the house? Is it one of those old historical homes?"

"It dates from the time of Queen Anne, ma'am. Do you have an interest in historical homes?"

He managed to divert her to a discussion of architecture, and escaped with his bachelorhood in good repair without alienating the mother. He noticed that Gordon did not accompany them, but followed in his own carriage. This looked like a maneuver to leave him and Cathy alone, as indeed it was. Lady Lyman was awake on all suits.

The mama's questions certainly indicated her thinking, and he felt he must inform Cathy how matters stood. "I wish I could spend more time at Pargeter," he said, "but as I shall be returning to Spain soon, I thought it best not to interfere with Cousin Paul's handling of the estate."

She appeared unperturbed by this. "I expect you are waiting for your leg to heal. How is it coming along?"

"Very well, and so is my head. Your plaster is scarcely necessary. I would leave tomorrow if it were not for this job Castlereagh has asked me to undertake for him. The sawbones feels I should give the bone a chance to heal. He wants me to stay in England until the spring." That left the whole winter to avoid entanglement, and he added awkwardly, "I may leave sooner. Any day now, as soon as this matter at the Horse Guards is settled."

She turned to him in the carriage and said bluntly, "You must not pay any attention to Mama. She is the same with all my callers. I have not set my cap for you, if that is what you fear."

"My dear Miss Lyman!" he said, and laughed nervously. "I do not consider myself such a prime parti as that, I promise you."

"Of course not," she agreed with alacrity. "You are only a younger son, but when one's daughter is pushing five and twenty, mothers become less demanding."

"Well then, as we are being quite frank—and I do like frankness in such dealings as this—I shall tell you I lied. Pargeter is twenty-five-hundred acres of prime cattle land."

"I shan't tell her," Cathy said, and laughed, but it was not precisely a happy laugh.

"That clears the air!"

"Did anything interesting happen at the Horse Guards today?" she asked, to show him in what light she considered this outing.

"Harold Leonard is beginning to trust me a little, I think. He gave me a not very important letter to handle this morning, as he was not feeling up to it himself. He has developed what might be a flu and went home early. Mr. Burack was not entirely happy at my actually being given a letter to deal with. Lord Cosgrave flew into a passion over something or other and heaved his ink pot at the wall."

"And Lord Costain?"

"He handled the not very important letter—a request from the Cabinet for certain information—then sat memorizing the list of procedures to be followed regarding sensitive documents. In the seemingly unlikely event of my ever being handed one, I shall know exactly what to do with it. How did Gordon's day of sleuthing go?"

"He has fallen in love with Mrs. Leonard," she said.

"With Mrs. Leonard! He must like older ladies. I am amazed. Her husband is a dull old stick. I made sure she would be an antidote."

"*Au contraire!* Gordon says she is a diamond of the first water, which means she is not actually old or ugly."

"If he has discovered anything to her discredit, we must make the most of it, to keep him from imagining he is in love with her."

She looked at him in surprise. "I expected more sense from you, a reader of Byron, Lord Costain! A whiff of sin will only make her irresistible. We must use the Spartan's trick."

"Dunk him in cold water, you mean?"

"Flutes," she declared. "The Spartans had such a natural inclination for war that they were played flute music to soothe their ardor. Gordon has such a natural inclination for romance and intrigue that we must dull his appetite by making Mrs. Leonard respectable. Not that I mean to say she is not," she added hastily. "I know nothing of the lady."

"Nor do I, but I know her husband, and if Mrs. Leonard is like him, I cannot think Gordon is in any danger."

The assembly was in full swing when they arrived. Lady Martin had decorated her lofty saloon with fur boughs and red velvet swags, in honor of the approaching season. The ladies' pastel gowns of spring had darkened to russets and greens and burgundies.

She was thrilled to have caught Lord Costain in her net, and peered to see what lady accompanied him. The face seemed familiar, but she could not put a name to it.

"Allow me to present Miss Lyman," Costain said.

"Miss Lyman? Not Sir Aubrey's little girl? I met you *eons* ago in France. You would not remember."

Costain saw the flush of embarrassment on Cathy's cheek, to have her antiquity flaunted.

"Yes, I remember," Cathy said. "It was just at the turn of the century, I think, at a New Year's levée, where they allowed the youngsters to participate."

"So you are Cathy Lyman," Mrs. Martin said, and studied the lady with a coolly appraising eye.

"All grown up now, and most charmingly, don't you think?" Costain said.

"Indeed! And how is your mama, Miss Lyman?"

"In very good health, ma'am. I shall tell her you were asking for her."

They went into the dancing room, where a waltz was in progress. Costain looked uncertainly at Cathy, wondering if he dare tackle a waltz. His leg had been causing him some pain since his adventure in St. James's Park. He felt he could pass muster in a square set, but one's faux pas would be more noticeable to his partner in a waltz.

She leveled a slightly annoyed look at him. "No, the patronesses of Almack's have not given me permission to waltz," she said, "for there was no such dance when I made my bows."

His mobile brows rose. "And what dance was in fashion in the medieval ages, when you made your bows, ma'am?" he asked facetiously.

"We hopped around in circles to the beat of a

drum, for there were as yet no true musical instruments either."

"May I compliment you on your remarkable state of preservation, ma'am. You are a little older than I thought—and quite old enough to have polished those primitive manners."

"My advanced years must save me from reproach. In any case, I *will* waltz, since Mama went to the expense of having a dancing master in to teach Gordon."

"Not Cathy?" he asked.

It was the first time he had used her Christian name. She looked conscious, but did not rebuke or encourage him. "Naturally Gordon needed a partner," she said.

"You have a temper," he said, studying her with a lazy smile. "I wonder you did not show your claws at Lady Martin's prodigious memory. Pray, what have *I* done to deserve it?"

"Nothing, but you were going to."

"No, I wasn't. Allow me to make my own errors before unsheathing your claws. I shall no doubt give you ample opportunity before the evening is out. My concern was that I would make you a poor partner." He did not mention a reason, but gave one quick peep at his leg.

Cathy's hand flew to her lips. "Oh, your leg! I am sorry, Costain. You walk so well that I had forgotten all about it."

Costain brushed it aside, as he disliked to harp on his wound. "It is not my leg but my two left feet that make me hesitate. Anyhow, I am game if you are."

She drew her bottom lip between her teeth. "Are you sure?"

He said gruffly, "Come, we are wasting this delightful music."

He swept her into his arms, and they joined the waltzers. Cathy enjoyed the unusual sensation of being an object of attention. She knew it was her

53

escort who engendered the interest in herself, but she was happy with even second-hand attention. Costain waltzed well, especially when one remembered he had one stiff leg. The swirling music and the pirouetting crowd induced a sort of euphoria. This was how life should be. This was how she always thought it would be when she was young.

When Costain lowered his head and smiled, she felt for a fleeting moment that he actually liked her. There was some special sparkle in his eyes. "I notice Lady Jersey frowning at you, Miss Lyman. She is not so sure your advanced years permit you the license of waltzing without her permission."

"Perhaps I should have worn my cap," she replied.

"No, a turban, I think—in five or ten years. You have the countenance for it. You must remember to add three feathers and a brooch. Feathers are like Capability Brown's trees. They come in threes. Two will not clump."

"That's not why they wear three. Three is a lucky number," she said. Cathy had always found this sort of badinage difficult, but the euphoria seemed to have spread even to her tongue.

"I am shocked at you for believing ignorant superstition, Miss Lyman. Everyone knows seven is the luckiest number. Mind you, the ladies would look like an ostrich's tail, carrying such a load of feathers. What a charming picture, though, a roomful of ostriches, waltzing about Lady Martin's saloon."

"You are too ridiculous!" She laughed.

He noticed the glow in her eyes, and felt culpable for encouraging her. What was merely banter to him seemed to be having the effect of flirtation on her, and he changed his manner accordingly.

"Have you spotted anyone who might be your intruder?" he asked.

Cathy came thumping back to earth. She had been too engrossed in Costain to even look, but she

54

did so then. All around her, gentlemen of roughly the right size and shape moved. But with so few clues to aid her, she could make no useful comparisons. "No," she said. "Perhaps Gordon is having better luck."

"We'll meet with him later. Let us just relax and enjoy the music now."

The evening lost its magic after that, but Costain behaved very properly. He came to her at the end of each set and introduced her to several eligible *partis*. She renewed acquaintance with some former friends, too, so the rout was enjoyable. Yet it did not satisfy her. Why did Costain introduce her to such old men? Two of them were widowers, and one had graying hair. Did he consider her too old for his own set? She was at least five years younger than he.

She was elated when a younger, handsome gentleman accosted them at the end of the cotillion. "Costain," he said with a smile. "May I have a dance with your charming partner?"

Seeing no reluctance in his partner, Costain said, "Certainly. Miss Lyman, this is my colleage, Mr. Burack. Mr. Burack, Miss Lyman."

While she made her curtsy, Cathy regarded Mr. Burack and did not dislike what she saw. He was a well-set-up young gentleman with hair the same chestnut color as her own. His eyes were a deep brown, and his smile was ready. His jacket was not so impeccably tailored as Costain's, but his physique did it more than justice.

They went off to join a set. "Have you known Costain long?" Mr. Burack asked.

"No, we are new acquaintances, sir. Is he an old friend of yours?"

"I never met him until last week, when he came to work for Cosgrave. Quite a war hero, I understand."

"Yes, he took a ball in the leg at Badajos."

"Odd, he dances so well," Burack said.

"It is healing nicely," she replied, and shot a gimlet look at Burack. She did not care for that remark. Was he suggesting Costain was malingering? "He is most eager to return to Spain," she added.

"I daresay he misses the excitement. We are a dull lot at the Guards. I wonder he bothered to join us."

"I expect Lord Costain is the sort of man who likes to be busy, and doing something for his country."

"Very admirable."

Yet Mr. Burack did not sound as if he admired Costain. In fact, she caught an intimation of resentment in his manner. Was it just jealousy of the ordinary man for the war hero? Or did he fear Costain would outshine him at the Guards as well?

Burack's next question put her on the alert. "How did you meet him?" he asked, and looked at her with brightly inquisitive eyes.

The cheek! "Our families are old friends, Mr. Burack," she said dampingly, and immediately changed the subject. "This is the first Christmas party of the season, I believe. What a lovely scent the fir boughs give to the room."

Mr. Burack wore the expression of a frustrated man, but his breeding forced him to discontinue his discussion of Costain, since the lady was so obviously opposed.

As the dance drew to a close he said, "May I do myself the honor of calling on you, Miss Lyman?"

"If you wish," she said with little enthusiasm.

"Where do you live?"

"On King Charles Street, not far from where you work."

"I see!" he said in a surprised voice.

As soon as the cotillion ended, Costain came forward. "Let us have a glass of wine," he said, and led Cathy away.

"He was *prying*, Lord Costain!" she exclaimed.

"Is it possible Mr. Burack is the one who is making trouble at the Guards?"

Costain looked interested in her suggestion. "Does he resemble your intruder?"

She had forgotten all about it, but she stopped at the doorway and looked back. She mentally pulled a hat low over Burack's face and drew a scarf up to nearly meet it. "I had the impression of an older, slighter man. Perhaps, with his shoulders hunched . . ."

"How about the voice?" Costain asked, warming to the idea.

"It did not sound similar at all, but the intruder consciously lowered his voice to frighten me."

"It is odd he made such a point of meeting you."

Again Cathy felt that shaft of annoyance. "Gentlemen do occasionally wish to be presented to me," she said.

Costain tilted his head and drew his bottom lip between his teeth. Then he laughed. "There! I told you you would have real cause to be angry with me before long. If it is any consolation, both Lord Duncan and Sir Andrew Longford asked me most particularly to be presented."

"It seems only age appreciates my charms," she said, not quite mollified, as the gentlemen mentioned were both nearing forty.

"Burack is no Methuselah," he said. She tossed her curls. "And Costain, at a mere nine and twenty, is coming to appreciate you, precocious fellow that I am."

"Let us go and see if Gordon has had any luck," she said, and they walked out.

Gordon came pacing from the refreshment parlor to meet them. Cathy rushed in with her suspicions of Burack.

"What did he say, exactly, to tip you the clue?" Gordon asked.

"He asked how long I had known Lord Costain, and how we met, and he mentioned it odd he danced so well when he was supposed to have wounded his leg."

"Upon my word, the fellow is a commoner," Gordon exclaimed. "He is either jealous as a green cow or he's our spy."

"He did sound a little jealous," Cathy allowed. Then she looked sharply at Costain. "I don't mean jealous because of me," she said. "Jealous of your title and your war record is what I meant."

"Counter jumper! He is nothing but a commoner in gentlemen's clothing," Gordon scoffed. "Never mind him. I have something of *real* interest to report, Costain."

He looked all around. The crowd was surging toward the refreshment parlor, where a line of servants were placing hot food on the table. The aroma of lobsters simmering in wine sauce floated on the air, mingling with the smell of hot roast beef.

"We'll find a quiet spot," Gordon said, and began pacing down the hall. He stopped at the library door and tossed his head to speed the others in joining him.

"What of supper? I am hungry," Cathy said as Costain hurried her along.

"Dash it, do you think being a spy is all waltzing and eating?" Gordon exclaimed. "I have been loitering about freezing corners with the wind rushing up my back all day long, following Mrs. Leonard. I have to impart my findings to Lord Costain."

"We'll eat later," Costain said with an apologetic look, and led Cathy into the library.

Chapter Six

Their thoughtful hostess had provided a decanter of sherry and glasses in the study in anticipation of wandering guests. Gordon went to the table near the blazing grate, poured, and handed the glasses around.

"Cheers and all that," he said, and crouched on the very edge of his chair, leaning toward Costain, who rested more comfortably on the sofa beside Cathy. Gordon's eyes gleamed with eagerness.

Costain was tired after a hard day's work and an evening of dancing. He settled in to enjoy the blazing hearth and the wine. The Lymans were obviously delighted with the vicarious excitement of it all. He could not see that they were in any real danger, and went along with it as if it were a game.

"What have you discovered, Gordon?" he asked.

"By the living jingo, Costain, you hit it on the head when you fingered Mrs. Leonard. She is in it up to her pretty neck. She is thick as thieves with every Frenchie in town."

"Indeed!"

"Yes, sir, a French modiste makes her gowns. That is Madame Marchand. A French milliner does her bonnets—Mademoiselle Dutroit, whose shop is right next door to Madame Marchand's. There is a regular clique of them. And she—Mrs. Leonard, I mean—also went to a toy store right across the street. They call themselves Whitfields, letting on they are English, but every second thing in the store is made in France. How do they get hold of it when we are at war with France? They have hand mirrors and perfume bottles and all those gaudy trifles you see on a lady's dressing table." Indignation turned him into a parody of his late father, and when he continued, his speech assumed an oracular quality. "It is infamous, letting the Frenchies infiltrate Bond Street to such an extent. You ought to look into it."

"Most ladies of fashion favor a French modiste, Gordie," his sister mentioned, peering to see Costain's opinion.

"*And* a French milliner? I ask you!"

"Mama bought her latest bonnet from Mademoiselle Dutroit. I wish I could afford the pretty red one in her show window. It has a huge black bow in front."

"You would look a quiz in that thing, Cathy. You need a face to carry off a bonnet like that. Besides, Mrs. Leonard bought it this very day. It suited her right down to the heels."

"It cost a fortune!" Cathy said. "She must be rich."

"If she is, she has money in her own right," Costain said, pensively rubbing his chin. "Harold Leonard has only a competence. He often complains of the cost of living in London. What sort of a lady is Mrs. Leonard?"

"A dasher of the first jet, Costain—good carriage, shiny black fur cape, shiny black hair, smooth white skin, dark eyes, and a stunning figure."

"She either has a patron, or she has money of her own," Costain decided. "Odd a young beauty would settle for Mr. Leonard, who has neither fame nor fortune to recommend him."

"We'll ask Mama," Gordon said. "She knows everyone, or she knows someone who knows everyone. Never guess it to see her now, but she and the Duchess of Devonshire was bosom bows. To this very day she receives a card from Prinny on her birthday."

As Gordon betrayed no particular infatuation with Mrs. Leonard, and as she appeared to be active enough to keep him fully occupied, Costain was much of a mind to let him continue following her.

"It is a pity Mr. Leonard came down with that flu, or we would have gotten a look at this Incomparable wife tonight," Cathy said.

Gordon looked at her in astonishment. "What the deuce are you talking about? She's here! Why do you think I have been lurking about the card room, when Miss Stanfield is here? I have been keeping an eye on Mrs. Leonard."

"She's here?" Cathy said, setting down her glass.

"Didn't I just say so?"

"Let us go and have a look at her," Cathy said, rising.

"There can be no harm in looking," Costain said, and rose reluctantly. "But don't call attention to yourself, Gordon. The spying business demands discretion."

Gordon laid his finger aside his nose. "Mum's the word," he said. "Sorry I can't introduce you to her. I have not managed to scrape an acquaintance, though I have spoken to her. She dropped a card—the ace of spades—and I picked it up for her. She said, "Thank you." She did forget herself and let out a few words of French to her partner. *N'est-ce pas*, I think it was."

"Everyone says that!" Cathy laughed.

"Yes, but she said it with an accent," he pointed out.

"Perhaps my working with her husband will has-

61

ten the acquaintance along," Costain said. "Leave it to me."

When they reached the refreshment parlor, Gordon pointed out the Incomparable. Mrs. Leonard was as he had described: a dashing brunette of a certain age, rouged, and highly adorned in jewelry. At her throat she wore a large rope of pearls, while a clutch of diamond brooches held a trio of feathers decorating her coiffure. Costain stared, and could hardly believe that dull old Harold Leonard was married to this dasher. If he was not quite old enough to be her father, he was not far from it. There was one seat vacant at her left side.

"I shall ask Lady Martin to seat me beside her," he said. "There are a couple of empty seats across the table. Why don't you take your sister there, Gordon?"

"Yes, by Jove. It is time for fork work. That roast beef is making my mouth water. Come along, Cathy."

Cathy gave her deserting escort a rebukeful look. "I hope you enjoy your supper, Lord Costain," she said, and left with a toss of her curls.

Conversation was not always audible across the table, for there was a loud buzz of talk and laughter, but Cathy overheard snatches of talk. She heard Costain introduce himself, and exclaim in well-simulated surprise that Mrs. Leonard was the wife of his colleague. "You are so young!" he said in admiring accents, then laughed that laugh of engaging diffidence with which she was familiar. "That was gauche of me," he continued. "One would think Mr. Leonard were Methuselah."

Mrs. Leonard flapped her long lashes at him. "You are forgiven, Lord Costain. I hear that sort of thing constantly. It is true there is a discrepancy in our ages, but I try to play the matron. Hence the feathers in my coiffure," she added coquettishly.

"But they are charming, Madame. *Très soignés.*"

How well he simulated compliments. Just so had

he smiled at her while they waltzed. A Mr. Hargrave on Cathy's left side engaged her in conversation. When she could harken to her eavesdropping again, she observed that Costain was sliding the occasional French phrase into his conversation.

"No, but it is early days yet. *Entre nous*, I am not eager to spend the holiday *en famille*. What will you be doing for Christmas, Mrs. Leonard?"

She must have asked him what he would do for Christmas. Her reply was in English only. "I should like to get Leonard away to the country for a week. Alas, no invitation has been forthcoming thus far. It is fourpence to a groat he would not go in any case. He is a demon for work, and I could not leave town without him."

"We at the Horse Guards are well aware of his work habits. He puts us all to the blush. But even God, you know, rested on the seventh day of his labors."

Cathy felt a poke at her elbow and turned to Gordon. "Is he trying to pump her for news or to seduce her?" Gordon hissed.

"Probably both," Cathy replied with an air of amused indifference.

Gordon's interest perked up at this lenient speech. "Daresay a spy has to resort to such methods. By Jove, I shall bear this lesson in mind."

"Don't you dare try anything with her, Gordie. She is much too old and too wicked for you."

After the supper, Gordon disappeared and Costain brought Mrs. Leonard to introduce to Cathy.

"Miss Lyman is an old friend of my family's," he said to Mrs. Leonard. "Cathy, I would like you to meet Mrs. Leonard. Her husband and I are colleagues."

The ladies exchanged a smiling curtsy. "Was that darling boy beside you your brother, Miss Lyman?" Mrs. Leonard asked.

"Yes. Do you have any family, ma'am?" Cathy

inquired, to remind Costain of the lady's married status.

"Alas, I am not so fortunate, but I have a darling little pug who is all in all to me. I call her May, for she came to me on May Day. She is a Taurus, like myself. An earth sign. So kind and gentle, unless attacked, of course. Then she becomes quite vicious. She dotes on the arts, especially music. We have that in common. Are you interested in the horoscope?" She looked with bright interest to her listeners. Both disclaimed any knowledge of this art.

"Most fascinating," she said. "I live by the stars. They told me of May's fondness for music. When my little doggie is out of sorts, I play the pianoforte for her. She especially enjoys the new waltz."

Cathy hardly knew how to reply to such a foolish outburst. "I have a kitten," she said.

"I had one, but May was jealous. I had to give her away." Mrs. Leonard then turned to Costain to inquire for his sign. Upon learning that he was born in October, she smiled in satisfaction. "I thought as much! A Leo. A natural leader," she said, and continued with various compliments.

She did not inquire for Miss Lyman's birth sign. When the music resumed, Mrs. Leonard sighed forlornly and said, "I daresay it is back to the card parlor for me. You youngsters run along and enjoy the dance."

Costain took the hint and asked her if she would stand up with him. "I really should not dance when poor Leonard is ill, but perhaps just once," she said. "I hope it is true what I have read, that people admire us for our virtues, but like us for our faults. I am deep dyed in faults."

Naturally Lord Costain took objection to this wholesale self-condemnation. "I find that hard—no, impossible—to believe. Your husband speaks most highly of your forebearance."

By some invisible sign Costain summoned a friend to take Cathy off his hands, and he disappeared with Mrs. Leonard. At the dance's end he returned to Cathy without his partner. Cathy was unaccountably furious with his satisfied smile and asked in a stiff voice if he would mind taking her home now, as she had a slight headache.

"You can always return if you dislike leaving early," she added with a glance across the room at the lady he would be returning to.

"I've gone as far as decency allows on first acquaintance," he replied, not pretending to misunderstand her.

"I wager you have."

He made his adieu to the hostess and called for the carriage at once. Gordon decided to remain at the assembly to try for a dance with Miss Stanfield.

"Do you really have a headache, or only a fit of pique?" Costain asked as they drove home.

"Am I not entitled to a headache after being slighted in public?" she asked. "Do you think no one noticed my escort deserted me at dinner, and made me look a fool?"

"We went to the assembly to see what we could discover. Mrs. Leonard was the best lead we came across."

"I wonder if Mr. Burack was not a better lead," she replied.

"I see him every day. If we had remained behind, we could have seen whether he stood up with Mrs. Leonard. That would have been interesting. It is odd he did not approach her all evening. He has been at the Guards longer than I. He must have met her before now. Their not exchanging so much as a glance looks suspicious."

"You must ask her about Burack when you call on her," Cathy said, wearing a face of determined disinterest.

"It will be better to let Gordon continue his watch. I wonder—perhaps we should sic him on to Burack instead. It is pretty clear Mrs. Leonard is no spy."

What was clear to Cathy was that Lord Costain was easily duped by a pretty flirt.

"I suggest you take a bone for May when you call on Mrs. Leonard, Lord Costain," she said with a knowing look. "I fear the way to that lady's heart is through her pug."

"You read me like a book, ma'am. I shall ask Cook to save me a steak bone."

They proceeded in silence for a few blocks. The only sound in the carriage was the echo of the hooves and wheels coming through the windows.

As they turned in at King Charles Street, Cathy said, "Did you discover where Mrs. Leonard gets her money? That was an expensive-looking cluster of diamonds she was wearing."

"One can hardly ask such an intimate question on first acquaintance."

"Perhaps when you get to know her better . . ."

The carriage drew up in front of the house and stopped. "I shall take you in," he said. "Don't be concerned if you see my carriage waiting outside. I want a word with Gordon. He said he would not be long."

"Very well."

He escorted her to the door. Before opening it, he said, "I don't know what tomorrow may bring. Can you leave the evening open in case something comes up?"

Leaving an evening open was never any problem for Cathy, but she did not precisely say so. "We often have an evening at home during the dull winter months. I believe tomorrow evening is free."

She thought Costain would smile and at least pretend to be pleased, but he was frowning at the door knocker. "You wouldn't happen to have a book on astrology in that study?"

"I shouldn't think so. It is all foolishness, you know."

"I know, but I seem to remember someone telling me I was a Libra. Mrs. Leonard said I was a Leo."

66

"You mean she is shamming it? Why would she boast of expertise in such an idiotic thing as astrology if it is not true?"

"Perhaps because it *is* an idiotic thing. It half convinced me the lady is a fool. That and her near adoration of a dog."

Cathy bit her lip. "You mean she wants us to think she is a ninnyhammer—and that suggests she is as sly as a fox. I shall ask Rodney about astrology. He knows everything. Everything perfectly useless, I mean."

"You were angry with me for flirting with her, but it was all in the way of business, you know," he said with a teasing smile.

"I was not angry because of that! I just felt ridiculous when you went hounding off to sit with her at dinner and foisted me onto Gordon in front of everyone. A lady has her pride, you must know."

He lifted a lazy eyebrow. "So has a gentleman, Miss Lyman. You might at least pretend to a proper fit of pique."

"I think you mean jealousy, milord."

"If you insist on calling a spade a spade."

"I do, and I insist on calling embarrassment by its proper name, not jealousy."

"When a gentleman embarrasses a lady, he must be in error, and I apologize. I shan't do it again."

"That is quite all right. I realize business comes before pleasure."

"Good. Then you do realize it would have given me more pleasure to have been your supper partner. I was never much good at paying insincere compliments. It wearies me."

"Then why do you bother?" she snipped.

"Because Mrs. Leonard expected them."

"Oh, Mrs. Leonard!"

"Good Lord! You didn't think I was merely flattering *you.* Really, Miss Lyman, I thought we had a better understanding than that."

As their understanding was that they went out

together in the way of business, and he had no romantical interest in her, she hardly knew how to
reply.

After a moment she said, "He does have a book
on astrology. Uncle Rodney, I mean. I remember
noticing it on the shelves. It is a horrid cheap book
with a red cover, all painted with little symbols.
Rams and goats and things. I shall check it this
very instant. Only think, if she is shamming it,
Lord Costain, then—"

She came to a frowning pause. "Then what? How
could she possibly have access to any state secrets?
Mr. Leonard would not be allowed to take documents from the office, surely? He would have to copy
them at work, and that means he is working with
her."

"Or someone at the office is. You have not forgotten Mr. Burack, who tried to pump you for news,
and so carefully avoided the lady all evening? There
are other gentlemen as well. I only mention Mr. Burack, as you know him."

"It will be best for Gordon to continue watching
Mrs. Leonard. If you are not a Leo, I mean," she
added, and laughed that so important a matter
should hang by such a slender thread.

"You must let me know my sign tomorrow. I shall
drop by in the afternoon, if I may? Say about four,
just in time for tea."

"Mama will like that," she said unthinkingly.

Costain was a little surprised that Miss Lyman
did not show greater pleasure. But then, he had
gone out of his way to let her know there was nothing serious between them, so he had to pretend to
approve her lack of enthusiasm.

He opened the door and she went in with a casual
wave. "I don't have to bother with the formality of
assuring you I had a delightful evening, do I?"

"Certainly not, ma'am. That is one of the few
perquisites of our position. We need not pretend to
nonexistent pleasure. In the interest of dispassion-

ate truth, however, I should like to say that *I* enjoyed myself."

"Tell Mrs. Leonard," she said, and closed the door with a quizzing smile, while Costain frowned in dissatisfaction.

That was not what he meant! That was not his meaning at all. He enjoyed Miss Lyman's company. It was unusual to be with a young lady who was not constantly throwing her bonnet at him. She was peeved that he had deserted her for dinner in front of the crowd, and who could blame her? It was a farouche thing for him to have done. Any other lady would have been in the boughs for hours.

Miss Lyman merely told him he had made her feel awkward, and that was an end of it. When he tried to flirt a little to make up for the lapse, she paid not the slightest heed. She was thinking of the case all the while, as he ought to have been doing himself. Mrs. Leonard ... Was that a lead worth following? If she was wangling state secrets from someone, he doubted very much it was her husband. Mr. Burack was more like it. And if she was using an affair with him to discover secrets, might she not be interested in another channel into the Horse Guards as well?

His mind skimmed lightly over various possibilities until Gordon's carriage was heard approaching, at which time he got out of his rig and went to meet him.

"Oh, you're still here, Costain. Waiting for me, are you?"

"I want to ask you something. Did Mrs. Leonard stand up with Burack after I left?"

"No, she left shortly after you. Now that you mention it, though, he left soon after her."

"I see!"

"You think there is something between them?"

"It's possible."

"So, who am I to follow tomorrow?"

"Mrs. Leonard, and do it discreetly. She has seen

you with Cathy now, and she knows I am Cathy's friend. We don't want her getting any ideas of collusion."

"I shall hire a hansom cab to loiter at the corner of Half Moon Street and follow her if she leaves. Naturally I shall wear a new disguise as well. I'll get into the attic and dig out a beard and some old clothes. And spectacles. We used to have some dandy plays when Papa was alive. How shall I contact you if I am not to go to your office?"

"I shall be coming for tea tomorrow. Can you be here at four?"

"I shall, if Mrs. Leonard is behaving herself. If I am hot on her trail, I shall try to get a note to you."

"Excellent. I appreciate your help."

"It was me who put you on to Mrs. Leonard," he said modestly, forgetting who had originally suggested watching her. "Daresay you might not have tumbled to her in a dog's age."

"I believe Cathy is waiting for you inside. Ask her about Leo," he said with an air of mystery that he thought would appeal to young Lyman.

"Is that our code word for Mrs. Leonard?"

"No, for Costain."

"Eh?"

Costain winked, tipped his hat, and got into his carriage.

Gordon was not slow in darting into the house to speak to Cathy.

Chapter Seven

Gordon strode into the study and peered around the room to ensure they were alone. "What have you got to tell me about Leo?" he asked in sepulchral accents.

Cathy looked up from the book she was perusing and said triumphantly, "He is not a Leo at all; he is a Libra. You know what *that* means!"

Gordon hadn't the slightest notion what she was talking about, but tried to make sense of it. After a frowning pause he said, "Are you telling me Lord Costain is not Lord Costain? Who the devil is he? Ah-ha! Lovell!"

"Of course he is Lord Costain, Gordon, but he was born in October."

"October, eh? Er, what of it? I mean to say—"

"It means he is not a Leo."

"What is his Christian name, then, and what difference does it make anyhow?"

She explained the situation and Gordon soon understood her point. "So Mrs. Leonard is puffing herself off as an astrologer when it is nothing of the sort. I wonder now, is May actually a Taurus?" he asked suspiciously.

"Yes, if the dog was born in May, as she says, it is a Taurus, and so, one must assume, is Mrs. Leonard. Not that it matters. Someone probably told her she was a Taurus. I know I am a Gemini, though I have no interest at all in astrology. One knows these things. She told that story only to make us think she was a goosecap."

"One thing she did not lie about was her fondness for the demmed dog. It goes everywhere with her, nipping at pedestrians and squealing its dashed head off. She has made it a fur coat and a toque—a *French* hat," he added as this occurred to him.

After more discussion of Mrs. Leonard's slyness, Cathy asked how matters had gone with Miss Stanfield, and Gordon announced stoically that he had refused an invitation to tea the next afternoon. "Well, as good as an invitation. I was standing right beside Lord Harcourt when she invited him, and she looked at me, too. I feared she would not like it above half when I told her I was busy, but I think my refusal piqued her interest. She invited me to call one day soon. I told her I am pretty busy. I mean to say, I cannot go calling in a wig and rusty old suit. Leo wants me to wear a disguise. It is a good notion to refer to Costain as Leo, just between ourselves."

"He is not a Leo; he is a Libra."

"Dash it, you can't call a fellow Libra. That ain't a name. Anyone listening would suspect a trick straight off. What is my sign? I was born the end of November."

"Sagittarius," Cathy told him after glancing at the book.

"That's out. I'll be demmed if I'll have anyone calling me Sagittarius."

They soon went upstairs. Lady Lyman was an early retirer. She did not receive an account of the rout until the next morning at breakfast. She was satisfied with the outing, and more than satisfied to learn that Lord Costain would come to tea that afternoon. When she began to speak of a June wedding, Cathy informed her that Costain planned to return to the Peninsula as soon as possible, and turned the conversation to Mrs. Leonard.

"Do you know anything about her, Mama?" she asked.

"What was her maiden name?"

"I don't know."

"You must remember, dear, my memories are some years old. Very likely she was still a Miss when I knew her. I do not recall a Mrs. Leonard."

"She is about thirty-five, so she would perhaps have been making her bows when you were in London." She described the lady, but Lady Lyman declared that she had known a dozen young brunette beauties.

"If you can discover her maiden name, no doubt I shall be able to help you. Meanwhile I shall inquire for a Mrs. Leonard of my friends. If she is anyone, someone will know her. Now, about you and Costain, my dear. As he plans to return to Spain, we must think in terms of a winter wedding. He will want to ensure having a child on the way before leaving. You must come home for your accouchement, Cathy. That explains his interest in you. I thought it rather odd, but he is in a rush, poor lad. I do hope he returns safely from Spain. And in case he does not, you must have a son. A daughter is no good to you. She will not inherit Pargeter. You do not want to be stuck in a Dower House."

"I don't believe he plans to marry before leaving, Mama," Cathy said.

"Very properly said, my dear. A lady never thinks she is being courted until she has received her proposal. Do you think—a small wedding, or a large one?"

"Let us not make any plans at all, Mama."

Lady Lyman nodded her agreement. "A quiet

wedding, then. Perhaps that is best, considering the season. One cannot like to ask guests to travel over icy roads. I do hope the duke and duchess will come!"

"No plans, Mama. I have promised Uncle Rodney to make a fair copy of chapter five," Cathy said, and escaped to the study.

Uncle Rodney was not yet out of bed, which allowed Gordon to use his office to transform himself into an elderly man with a gray beard, spectacles, a rusty old black coat, and his uncle Rodney's blackthorn walking stick.

"I would not recognize you in a million years," Cathy said when he doddered out, tapping the floor with his cane, as if checking his path for impediments. "Can you see with those spectacles? They make your eyes look huge."

"I have to lift 'em up to see," he said. "I tried on that old pinch-nez of Papa's, but it kept falling off, and with the walking stick in one hand, it was too much bother. Wouldn't I love to call on Charlie Edison in this getup!"

"Will you be home at four to meet Lord Costain?"

"Of course I shall. It's me he's coming to see. He most particularly asked me to be here."

Cathy accepted this with apparent good humor. What did she think, that Costain was coming to pay court to her? She set about the tedious chore of writing a fair copy of her uncle's translation of Schiller. It was heavy going, and virtually meaningless to her. The only sound in the study was the scratching of her pen, and the low, steady wind howling through the streets. Occasionally the wind would find a handful of leaves uncovered by the snow, and hurl them against the window, causing a momentary panic.

She wrote all morning without other interruption, and was happy when a caller stopped by in the afternoon. Mr. Holmes was a regular customer. He was translating a book of poetry, *Les Jardins* by Jacques Delille, from French into English. His own French was spotty. He wanted the exact literal translation, which he would put into poetical language.

At a quarter to four she was interrupted by another tap on the door. When she opened it, Lord Costain was blown in on a gust of wind. His nose was red, his cheeks were rosy, and his dark eyes gleamed with youthful spirit and health.

"What a day! One would think we were in Canada. I pity poor Gordon his vigil." He wiped his feet on the mat and came into the warmly inviting study. A cozy fire blazed in the grate. A welter of books lay open on tables and shelves. "I hoped you might be here. We can have a private word before joining your mama. How cozy you look, Miss Lyman, with the signs of your profession scattered about you."

She put a finger to her lips. "Uncle Rodney is in his office. I'll close the door." She did this as Costain removed his outer garment.

"Who is there? Is it for me?" Rodney asked.

"No, Uncle. It is a friend of mine. I shall close your door so we don't disturb you."

"Is it not time for tea yet?"

"Very soon," she said, drawing the door shut.

When she returned, Costain had taken up the book of French verses left by the poet. "French verse," he said, lifting his delicate brows in surprise. "Somehow that surprises me. I did not take you for a romantical lady."

"We cannot all be romantics. I am translating it for a client," she said, damping down a sting of resentment.

"Is there a blue stocking hiding beneath that charming gown, Miss Lyman?" he asked lightly.

"Certainly not. One wears woolen hosiery in such

dreadful weather as this, and it does not come in the lively colors of silken hosiery."

"You take me too literally."

"I know what you meant. I am no Bluestocking. I give only a rough literal translation. It will be for my client to polish it into a gem worthy of study."

"May I?" he asked, taking up her translation and glancing at it. He read it slowly, with an occasional nod of appreciation. "I should take a close look at the translation when it comes out if I were you. You have used some elegant similes here."

"No, Monsieur Delille used them. I have only translated," she insisted, but she felt a glow of pleasure at his praise. She picked up the book on astrology and opened it to show Costain.

"Shall we sit by the fire and be comfortable?" he suggested. Taking the book, he led her to the sofa.

"When is your birthday, milord?" she asked.

"The thirteenth of October. You are too late to buy me a present this year. But next year, if we are still—friends—you might send me a trinket to the Peninsula. A block of ice, perhaps. That would be appreciated there. But I see you becoming impatient with my nonsense. It serves me right for trying to cadge a gift from you. Am I a Leo?"

"Certainly not. You are a Libra, sir. And Mrs. Leonard is a sly minx," she declared.

"Let us temper our ire with common sense. Perhaps she is just a lady with that dangerous thing Pope warns us of—a little learning. Was your mama able to tell you anything about her?"

"Not yet. She will make inquiries among her friends. Is there anything new at the Horse Guards?"

"Mr. Leonard is back at work. I discovered his wife's name is Helena. I mentioned having met her last night, you know. After a little discreet hinting, I discovered they have been married only a few years. Both have been married before. He is as proud of her as if she were a queen. He just shakes his poor grizzled head and says he doesn't know what she saw in him. No more do I, nor anyone else with an eye in his head."

"Mama asked me to discover her maiden name if possible."

"I shall try and see if I can discover it."

"Is your acquaintance with Mr. Leonard intimate enough that you could hint about the source of her jewelry?"

"No, but he implied that her first husband had deeper pockets than he has himself. Perhaps he was the supplier of diamond brooches and pearl necklaces."

"No name was given for this first husband, either?"

"I am feeling my way into the territory carefully. One cannot crop out into an interrogation too quickly without sounding suspiciously curious."

She nodded. After a short pause she asked, "Is Mr. Burack behaving himself?"

He cast a knowing glance at her. "I wondered how long it would take you to inquire for him. I caught him in my office, ostensibly looking for a copy of a letter to Cosgrave from the Admiralty. He surely knows how unlikely it is that I would have been given such a thing. As a translator, you will realize that is French for telling you he was looking for something else."

She sat a moment, thinking, then said, "As he realizes you are not given access to sensitive information, perhaps he was searching for a billet-doux to—or from—Mrs. Leonard," she suggested with an innocent look. "If he is her beau, and the source of her income, he might be jealous of you."

"We are calling this spade by its proper name, I see. It could be that. I have a different idea. I received a personal letter from Spain today, from a military friend, asking after my health. Burack might have seen the frank, or he might have learned from the mail boy that I had received it. I

77

don't usually receive personal mail at work, but I had written to my friend some time ago of Castlereagh's offer, and that I planned to accept."

"And you think Burack mistook the letter for a business matter. Was it in your office?"

"No, I put it in my pocket, to take home and write an answer this evening. I didn't mention the letter to him at all. If he knows of it, it was because he is very much on the qui vive as to what passes in the office. Such devotion to one's work is uncommon. Especially at the Horse Guards," he added with a weary look.

"You look fagged, Costain. Perhaps you are over-exerting yourself. You need your tea."

It was so cozy by the grate, and so pleasant being cosseted a little by Cathy, that Costain was reluctant to leave. "I don't suppose we could have the tray brought in here?" He watched as her eyes widened in dismay. "Was that very indiscreet of me? I meant no harm—your uncle is right next door."

"It—it is just that Mama has prepared things in the other room," she said, feeling foolish. Her mama considered this tea party a great occasion, and had taken pains with it. Cathy's own inclination was to remain exactly where they were, with her uncle's door closed. "I shall call Uncle, and we'll all go in together."

Costain looked at his hat and coat but left them where they were. It occurred to Cathy that he would have to return here before leaving, but it never entered her modest head that he left them where they were on purpose to be alone with her.

She tapped on Rodney's door and he came out. "Ah, Lord Costain, come calling on our Cathy again, eh?" He said no more, but the roguish shake of his head denoted total understanding and approval. "I hope Cook has made her hot scones," he said. "There is nothing like a hot scone on such a day as this."

He looked in vain for his hot scones. To impress

Cathy's beau, Lady Lyman had arranged a formal lunch of cold meat and cheese and bread. It was taken not before the warm grate, but in the drafty dining room, with every spare servant in the house standing ready to pass plates and fill cups. The dark paneling in the room absorbed the last rays of sunlight at the windows, and the lamps were placed so highly on the wall that they scarcely reached the dining board. It was like eating in a cave. The conversation, consisting mostly of probing questions from Lady Lyman and vague replies by Costain, was stilted.

There were two themes to vary the conversation. Lady Lyman occasionally gave a *tsk* of annoyance and wondered where Gordon had gone on such a wretched, cold day. At regular intervals Rodney regretted the absence of hot scones.

As the room was so chilly, they took their tea to the saloon to finish up there. As soon as decently possible after tea, Costain rose to take his leave. "Why don't you see Lord Costain to the door, Cathy?" Lady Lyman suggested with an arch look.

She accompanied him from the saloon and into the study. "I must apologize for Mama's curiosity," she said, trying to sound calm.

"I am accustomed to the rampant curiosity of mamas," he replied. "It is her other concern that also concerns me. Where the devil is Gordon? He was supposed to meet me here at four."

Before Costain had put on his greatcoat, the door flew open and an elderly gentleman wearing a gray beard and spectacles staggered in. His spectacles were frosted from the weather to further impede vision, and he tripped over the edge of the carpet.

"Is that you, Leo?" he asked, and ripped off the spectacles.

"What kept you?" Costain asked.

"You'd best have a seat, for what I have discovered will knock you over," Gordon announced.

Casting off his outer garments, he sank gratefully onto the sofa before the fire to regain his breath before opening his budget.

Chapter Eight

As soon as he had recovered his breath, Gordon rose, swelling with triumph. "Mrs. Leonard has a French lover," he announced, and waited for praise that did not come. Were it not for Cathy's gasp of surprise, his stunning announcement would have fallen flat. Lord Costain's eyebrows may have risen marginally, but they were well-arched brows, and the motion was hardly sufficient to reward Gordon for his effort.

"Are you sure he is French?" Costain asked.

"If he is not a Frenchie, it is more than I know, for she met him in rooms above the French milliner's shop."

"How do you know? Did you follow her into the shop?" Cathy asked.

"After cooling my heels for twenty minutes after she went inside, I went to the window and peered in—with those curst spectacles off. I could see plain as glass she wasn't in there, so I went in, pretending I wanted a bonnet for my granddaughter. I had to buy you a bonnet, Cathy."

"What is it like?" she asked with considerable interest.

"An ugly old black round bonnet, the cheapest thing Mademoiselle had in her shop, which don't mean it was cheap. Decked out with a black veil, it will do for a funeral. I had to buy something for an excuse to linger. I can say for a certainty Mrs. Leonard was not there."

"Are you quite certain she didn't suspect you were following her, Gordon?" Costain asked. "If she was aware of it, she may have gone in by the milliner's front door and out the back to evade you."

"I am dashed certain of it. I followed her only a few blocks. She did not leave her house until two o'clock, and she went straight to Dutroit's. She did not spot my hansom cab in the morning, for I used a hundred ruses to fool her. Parked it at the corner where she could not see it, and drove around from time to time. Around noon I even changed carriages. Why would she feel it necessary to evade me if she were not up to something suspicious?"

"She was obviously evading you," Costain conceded, "but that does not necessarily mean she is a spy. An adulterous wife usually takes some pains to keep her secret. If this is her regular way of carrying on, she might fear that her husband is having her followed. Not that Mr. Leonard seems a suspicious sort," he added pensively.

"Perhaps the wife of her lover is having her followed," Cathy suggested.

Costain smiled his approval. "Trust a lady to think of that. You didn't get a look at the man she met?" he asked, turning to Gordon.

"No, but when it go to be four o'clock and they had still not come out, and I had this appointment with you, I left the carriage and went to the rear of the shop, looking for a back door. A hired hansom cab was just leaving. I could not like to run after it and show them I was not an old man, so I just watched it fly away, but Mrs. Leonard was in it with a man. I know it was her even if I didn't see her face, for she was wearing the red bonnet with the black ribbon. Daresay she was planning to meet up with her own carriage somewhere else and drive home nice as a nun with another new bonnet. I dashed straight home to report to you, Leo. Oh, and the man was fattish."

"You have done excellent work, Lyman," Costain said. But common sense told him that if Mrs. Leonard had a lover, it probably had nothing to do with the business at the Horse Guards. She was a youngish, attractive lady married to an older man. Adultery, in such cases, was not uncommon. No doubt they would eventually discover her marriage had been arranged by her family against her wishes.

"I shall keep on her trail and see if I can get a closer look at the man next time," Gordon said. "Pity he drove a hired hack, or I might have recognized his prads. I recognize most of the teams around town."

"Best change your disguise, in case she saw you behind the shop when they were leaving," Costain mentioned.

"That'll be a relief," Gordon said with great feeling. "I shan't be an old man next time. I might be a footman. One sees them everywhere. They are as common as belly buttons."

Cathy said, "What you should be is a woman, then you could loiter about such places as milliner's shops without exciting curiosity."

"If you think I am going to be seen in public in a dress, let me tell you, you have another think coming! How would *you* like it?"

"I would like it fine." Cathy laughed. "What you probably mean is how would I like to be seen in public in trousers. I shouldn't mind that, either. If you did pose as a lady, you could wear that round bonnet you bought. I don't want it. Where is it, by the bye?"

"Why it's—" He looked all around. "Demme, I must have left it in the hansom cab. Pity." He turned to Costain. "Have you discovered anything of interest, Costain?"

Costain mentioned Burack's search of his desk.

"I shouldn't be in the least surprised if it was Burack that Mrs. Leonard was meeting, with his coat stuffed to look fat."

"I would be very much surprised," Costain said. "He did not leave the office. Cosgrave was out at a meeting or some such thing, and Burack was in his office, working on his correspondence from two to four, when I left."

"And besides, Burack is not French," Cathy pointed out.

"He don't *admit* to being French," Gordon said. When this received a jaundiced look, he thought it best to drop the matter. "What are we doing tonight, Costain?" he inquired.

Society was thin in winter. Costain could not think of anyplace they might all go. Bearing in mind Lady Lyman's pressing questions, it seemed wise not to dance attendance on Cathy too assiduously.

"We have all earned a respite," he said, looking at Cathy.

She made the effort to accept it in good spirits. "That will give me an opportunity to catch up on my correspondence," she said.

"I daresay Mrs. Leonard is not brass-faced enough to be meeting her lover when her husband is at home," Gordon said. "I shall go to my club this evening, and keep a sharp eye out for those flat thumbs and squinty eyes while I am about it. Will you call at the same time tomorrow to receive my report, Costain?"

Costain knew the ineligibility of popping up each day for tea. "I shall be in touch, perhaps by letter," he said.

"But what if something urgent arises?" Gordon asked. "I mean to say, you don't want me running to you, and since that weasel of a Burack is reading your correspondence, I daresay you don't want me to write, either."

"Why don't I stop in for a moment after tea tomorrow on my way home?" he suggested. "I shall come here, to the office, to avoid disturbing the family."

His expression was politely bland, but Cathy easily read his thinking. "He is afraid of falling into parson's mousetrap," she said to herself. "You can meet Lord Costain here, Gordon," she said, to show him she had no intention of hounding him.

No one objected, and Costain soon took his leave. Gordon was peeved at Leo's lack of enthusiasm for his hard day's work and magnificent discovery.

"I don't think Leo appreciates what I have stumbled into," he grumbled. "A fellow like Costain—all he has on his mind is adultery. He never batted an eye at that woman's carrying on. You don't want to have too much to do with the likes of him, Cathy. Very wise, the way you arranged for me to meet him here tomorrow afternoon."

Cathy sighed and gazed into the grate. "You are right, Gordon. He doesn't care for me in the least."

"Damme, don't wheeze and mope like that. We will nab you a husband when I go to Italy. *If* I go to Italy," he added. "I have been thinking, this sort of work suits me down to the heels. After I've gotten Mrs. Leonard and her friends behind bars, I may speak to Cosgrave about a regular position."

"And then how shall I find a husband?" she asked. "I wish—oh, I wish we went out more. It was so pleasant at Lady Martin's assembly last night. It reminded me of the old days, when Papa was alive."

Gordon was feeling derelict at canceling the Italian plan. It was demmed hard on Cathy, sitting home with Mama and Rodney and their old cronies, when she was not quite over the hill yet. He really ought to make a bit of a push to land her a fellow, or she'd end up battening herself on him and Miss Stanfield when they got married.

"I'll tell you what," he said. "I shan't go to the club tonight after all. You and I shall go out on the town."

"Are you invited to any dos?" she asked hopefully, for Gordon had a more active social life than she.

"There are no dos worth going to in the dead of winter, but the theaters are open. I shall take you to a play. We can look about for our intruder there as well as at my club. We'll take the opera glasses and examine every eye and thumb in the place."

"Lovely! Let us see what is playing at the theaters."

As it was so close to dinnertime, Gordon changed into evening clothes, and Cathy went to her room to choose her gown. With that chill wind howling, she chose a long-sleeved gown of sarsenet, and a stylish but warm shawl of mohair. A pleasant flutter of excitement beat in her breast. It was sweet of Gordon to oblige her like this. She had no real fears that his enthusiasm for the Horse Guards would hold sway for long. He would soon tire of standing about in the cold, and come to appreciate Italy's more beneficent clime.

The greater disappointment was Costain's very obvious eagerness not to become entangled with her. Oh, he was polite about it, but he did not really care for her. If she occasionally caught a light of interest in his eyes, or if he said things that sounded flatteringly personal, it was just his way. As Gordon pointed out, he was accustomed to the somewhat loose morals of his class. Ladies, unless they were ancient, were for flirting with. He knew no other way to deal with them, but he was careful not to let his flirting get out of hand.

If her social life had not been cut short by Papa's death, she would be able to handle his sort. She would smile and return his sallies with a careless

86

insouciance, but such skills were not learned in a day. She would go on in her own stolid manner. She knew no other way to deal with him.

"I daresay Lord Costain has some urgent business at work," Lady Lyman decided when she learned of his defection. "I have set on the twentieth of December for our little rout, Cathy. We shall write up the cards this evening."

"Gordon has asked me to go to the theater with him tonight, Mama," Cathy said.

"What is playing, Gordon? Shakespeare?"

"Shakespeare?" Gordon scoffed. "Nothing of the sort. Who wants to listen to that antique chatter? It is all prithees and by-your-leaves. I had sufficient enough of that in the schoolroom, thankee."

"*Sufficient* is sufficient," Rodney informed him.

"Eh?"

"*Sufficient* is enough; you need not add *enough*." Gordon just shook his head. The old fellow had gone off the deep end at last. "What does sufficient mean?" Rodney asked.

"It means sufficient."

"It means enough, so you need not say *sufficient enough*. That is pointless tautology. If you have any hope of being a diplomat, you must learn to speak English."

"Then why am I studying Italian?" He turned to his mother. "There is a dandy farce at the Royal Coburg. That is where we are going."

"My dear, do you think it proper to take Cathy to the Surrey side of the Thames?"

"Dash it, we ain't going to live there. The whole town is talking about the new farce at the Coburg. No wonder she hasn't a beau to her name, when you keep her wrapped in cotton wool."

"Your sister has made an eminently suitable connection, Gordon. It is Lord Costain I am thinking of. He might dislike to think she is running about town like a hurly-burly girl."

"If Cathy is a hurly-burly girl, I am a monkey.

Costain ain't such a toplofty article as you seem to think, Mama. He knows a thing or two."

"Article?" she said, her color rising. "You call the Duke of Halford's son an *article*?"

Rodney scowled and said, "Learn to speak English, my lad. It is what distinguishes man from the animals. In the Foreign Office—"

"I ain't so sure I will be a diplomat after all."

"You might do your country a greater service by refraining," Rodney said with awful sarcasm.

The meal continued in this somewhat fractious manner. Before leaving for the theater, Cathy said, "By the bye, Mama, I have learned a little more of Mrs. Leonard. Her first name is Helena, and she was married once before."

"How long ago? What was the first husband's name?"

"I don't know."

"Helena," Lady Lyman said, furrowing her brow. "The name rings a bell. I might remember, given time. Remind me in the morning, dear. I don't know how it is, but my memory is leaking away on me day by day. It is better for the past than the recent present, however, so there is hope."

"Ask Rodney," Gordon suggested. "He hasn't lost his mind yet."

"Memory, dear," Lady Lyman pointed out. "The young are really very poorly spoken these days."

She closed the door on her youngsters and went to the saloon to prepare for an evening of cards with her close circle of friends, mostly diplomatic widows like herself. It was a Mrs. Leadbeater who remembered Helena Johnson.

"She made her bows the same year as my daughter, Anne. She had no fortune to speak of—two thousand, I think it was. Less than ten thousand ought not to be presented, unless it is a noble family. And she was certainly not noble, but very pretty and forthcoming. She nabbed an aging M.P. Fotherington was well enough off, but an unreliable sort. I seem to recall there was some scandal attached to his death. In fact, he committed suicide, if memory serves."

"What sort of scandal?" Lady Lyman inquired.

"I believe it happened abroad, so I am not familiar with the details, but I think it had to do with gambling debts. It was around 1802. He was sent to France—what could it have been?"

Lady Lyman ransacked her fading memory and came up with something. "The signing of the Peace of Amiens, perhaps?" she suggested. "We were the only country at war with France then. Boney had been trying to persuade the Russian emperor to form a League of Armed Neutrality with Prussia and some other countries. But then, the emperor, Paul the First I think it was, was assassinated before it came to anything. Nelson had a good success at Copenhagen, and we all thought the war would continue, but Britain was tired of it, and the peace was signed at Amiens." She looked hopefully to Mrs. Leadbeater.

"Fotherington must have been mixed up in it," the dame said, nodding. "Several M.P.'s went along to help out with clerical duties. Perhaps he was giving away secrets to the enemy for money to pay his debts. He never came back to London—we heard later he shot himself in the mouth to avoid the shame of prosecution." A collective frisson went around the table at the image this called up. "Helena disappeared from the face of the earth. I had not heard her name again until tonight."

"And she is married again, is she?" one of the ladies asked.

"Back, and married to a Mr. Leonard, at the Horse Guards," Lady Lyman said.

"I don't know any harm of the lady except that she is forthcoming," Mrs. Leadbeater said forgivingly. "I mean to say, it is not her fault if Fotherington went astray. Poor gel, left without a penny to fly with. I remember everyone felt sorry for her.

She was quite popular. That is my trick," she said, and scooped up the cards. "Your deal, Lady Lyman."

The card game continued, and the gossip turned to Lord Byron and Lady Caroline Lamb.

Chapter Nine

The Royal Coburg lacked the finer amenities of Drury Lane, but it had boxes, at least, and it was to one of them that Gordon planned to take his sister.

"What do you mean, they are all sold out?" he demanded when the ticket seller told him this was the case.

"I could let you have a place in the gallery."

"The gallery! My good man, I am with a lady!"

"Never mind, Gordon," Cathy said with a sigh of disappointment. "Perhaps you could buy a seat now for tomorrow night."

"Dash it, we have had the horses put to. We have crossed the demmed slippery bridge in this filthy cold weather. You cannot expect me to devote every night of the week to obliging my sister. You stay here, Cathy, I shall take a peek into the boxes. I know for a fact Edison and Swinton have a box, for they invited me to go snacks on it with them. They may be able to squeeze us in."

He nipped upstairs, and Cathy stood alone, feeling more conspicuous than she liked, with the crowd pouring in. The audience was a somewhat motley crew, but there was a good sprinkling of the ton arriving. Before long, Gordon was back.

"It is just as I thought. Edison insists we join him. There is only one empty seat in the box, but I shan't mind standing. Parker is bound to leave before half an hour. He cannot go a whole night without gambling. Come along. They are waiting for us. You know Edison and Swinton."

She recognized two of the young gentlemen who rose to make their bows as chums of Gordon's. Swinton insisted on giving up his seat in the front of the box to Cathy. Three other gentlemen were introduced, but in the confusion she did not catch their names. It felt a little strange to be completely surrounded by black jackets. Cathy feared her presence was restricting their merriment at first, for the most often heard speech was "Watch your language, my good man. There is a lady present."

The gentlemen soon forgot she was a lady and the box echoed with the boisterous sound of England's gilded youth, snickering, teasing, and abusing each other in language fit for an Irish chairman. The responsibility of behaving properly fell to her immediate partner, Edison. He was a portly blond with a round face, wearing a cravat that looked as if it had been put on with a pitchfork, and a jacket with padded shoulders. He civilly inquired if she was comfortable two or three times, and when she convinced him she was, his conversation dried up. He turned his glasses on the other boxes and forgot her.

Cathy feared he might fall over the railing when he discovered Miss Stanfield across the hall. In his excitement, he forgot not only his manners but the law of gravity as well. Cathy had to snatch at the tails of his jacket to keep him from tumbling out of the box.

The farce being enacted was an inane thing with less plot than shouting and running about, making faces at the audience. As the females wore daring gowns and the dialogue was not far from lewd, however, the gentlemen enjoyed it very much. Cathy soon became bored and turned her glasses on the other boxes.

She first examined Miss Stanfield, to discover what it was about her that had all the young gentlemen acting like moonlings. She was a petite blond lady with full cheeks, lustrous eyes, and a permanent pout. Her gown was a marvel of lace and ribbons, and her hair was tightly curled. She worked her fan very fetchingly, but for the rest, Cathy found nothing outstanding in her. She supposed it was some spoilt beauty like Miss Stanfield that Lord Costain would marry one day.

When she had looked her fill at Miss Stanfield, she turned her glass along to the next box, and the next, assessing the ladies' toilettes and the gentlemen's faces and shoulders. In the farthest box on her left, she discovered Mrs. Leonard, and spent some time examining her.

She really was something quite out of the ordinary. Her palely beautiful face was designed on classical proportions, but it was the expression that caught Cathy's interest. She was one of those rare ladies whose beauty is enhanced by repose. The evening before she had looked only pretty, but sitting so still in the shadowed box, she looked beautiful, and ineffably sad. Were it not for the diamonds glittering at her throat, she might have posed for a painting of the Madonna by some Renaissance master. She wore a plain dark gown that added more distinction than all of Miss Stanfield's embellishments. Cathy wished she had such countenance, such poise. Mrs. Leonard was accompanied by an elderly lady.

Cathy wondered if the chaperone might be French. She was about to nudge Mr. Edison and ask for the dame's name, when a black sleeve came forward from behind Mrs. Leonard, proffering her a box of bonbons. Cathy trained the glasses to see the man's face. Presumably it would be Harold Leonard. She discovered he was a completely undistinguished man with gray hair. He might have been her father. She espied another man beside the elderly man, and focused her gaze on him. This was more like it! She caught a gleam of black hair, and a handsome profile.

Then the younger man turned, and she recognized the unmistakable features of Lord Costain. He was sitting in Mrs. Leonard's box! How was it possible? No wonder he never gave herself a second look. What a perfect couple the two of them made. Cathy stared for a long time, then she nudged Mr. Edison's arm and said, "Who is the chaperone with the beautiful black-haired lady in the corner box? Do you recognize her?"

Mr. Edison trained his glasses in the proper direction and emitted a soft sigh of pleasure. "I haven't a notion, but the brunette is certainly an Incomparable. I shall ask Swinton. He might know."

A moment later, Edison leaned over and said, "He don't know the old lady, but the Incomparable is a Mrs. Leonard. The old duffer behind her is her husband. What a waste!"

"Thank you. I was just curious. I thought I recognized the chaperone."

"Swinton knows all the beauties. This one ain't exactly top drawer, but she has them all beat for looks. Caro Lamb is nothing to her."

"Yes," Cathy agreed, in a daze.

"I say, Miss Lyman, are you feeling all right?"

"I am fine, thank you," she said, and attempted a smile. She set her glasses in her lap, in case Costain should see her spying on him.

The shouting from the stage and the laughter of the audience whirled around her unheeded. Costain and Helena Leonard, together. What did it mean? Had he been fooling them all along? Why had he set Gordon the task of following her, since he made little of Gordon's startling discovery? As she sat, thinking, the answer came to her.

He was Helena's lover, and he had chosen this underhanded way of having her followed. He wanted to know if she was being unfaithful to her lover as well as to her husband. Well, he had found out, and it served him right!

At intermission she told Gordon what she had discovered. He elected to remain behind with her while their companions went out to strut the halls. It seemed at first that the Leonards and Costain were not going to leave their box. They had arranged for wine to be brought in. The four of them sat sipping their wine and chatting. Cathy and Gordon moved to the shadows at the rear of their own box and watched through their glasses. They noticed that the older lady talked to Mr. Leonard, while Costain entertained Helena. Occasionally Mr. Leonard said a word to them. Poor man. He did not suspect he had a viper in his bosom.

Suddenly Mrs. Leonard stood up. Costain rose and took her arm to lead her from the box. Mr. Leonard and the elderly female companion remained behind.

"Costain has been making fools of us!" Cathy said angrily. "He is her lover, and he suspects she has another. That is why he set you to watch her, to find out who the man is."

"We don't know that. You are jumping to conclusions. He wouldn't be brazen enough to join his lover and her husband. It has got to be innocent."

"He has the gall for anything. Why did Costain not tell us about this when you asked him what we should do tonight? He felt he was safe, since you told him you would be at your club, and I said I would stay home and write letters. I begin to wonder just why Cosgrave does not trust him with any important work, Gordie. Perhaps Lord Costain put that translation I did for him to some evil use. I have abetted the enemy."

"If you did, and I don't believe it for a moment, you were an innocent dupe. They won't lob off your head for that. I shall nip out and have a word with Leo," Gordon said.

"No! He must not discover we are on to him."

Gordon's youthful face pinched to slyness. "We'll play a covert game," he said. "I shall edge up close behind them and see if I can overhear what they are saying. Pity I left off my disguise."

Cathy felt a nearly overwhelming compulsion to go along with her brother, but common sense deterred her. One black jacket was much like another. Gordon might manage to overhear them without being noticed among the crush of black jackets, but a couple would be more noticeable.

"I cannot stay alone in the box, Gordon. Take me out to join Mr. Edison."

"I will then, but be quick about it. The intermission is half over."

They nipped smartly out into the corridor. If Mr. Edison was unhappy to be saddled once again with the chore of escorting Gordon's sister, he was too polite to show it. In fact, Cathy took the notion he was happy to have a lady to flaunt in front of Miss Stanfield. They strolled past Miss Stanfield and her court for the remaining length of the intermission. Mr. Edison was seized by an unfamiliar streak of jollity each time they drew near the Incomparable. Cathy's slightest remark set him off in peals of merry laughter.

"What a squeeze" is all she said, and he drew to a full stop just two yards from Miss Stanfield.

"Ha-ha, you are a regular jokesmith, ma'am. You have hit it on the head. A squeeze is exactly what it is. I feel like a lemon." His eyes veered off to see if he was being noticed.

"You will be happy to hear you do not look like one, Mr. Edison."

"I should hope I am not yellow! Ha-ha-ha. I may be a little green, but time will cure that."

96

"You are certainly full of juice at any rate."

"I should say so! You have hit it on the head. Just so long as you are not calling me sour." Again he peered toward the Incomparable.

She had moved away, and Mr. Edison suddenly lost all his hilarity. "Well, are you enjoying the performance?" he asked.

"Indeed I am." *Especially since leaving our box*, she added to herself.

Cathy kept her eyes peeled for Lord Costain and Mrs. Leonard, but did not see so much as a sign of them. The intermission was long, giving her time to see everyone in the corridor. They were not there. She could conclude only that they had left, and hoped that Gordon had contrived to follow them. When the warning bell sounded, Mr. Edison escorted her back to the box. As they struggled through the crowd, she spotted Mr. Burack. He seemed to be looking around for the rest of his party. He saw her and nodded, then continued his scan of the crowd.

As soon as Cathy was in her seat, her eyes flew across the hall to Mrs. Leonard's box. Only Mr. Leonard and the female companion were there. Cathy raised her glasses, and saw that Mrs. Leonard's wrap still hung over the back of her seat. She planned to return then.

Suddenly Gordon appeared at her side. He tapped Cathy on the shoulder and beckoned her to the back of the box. "Swinton's left. You can sit back here beside me and talk."

She gave one last look to the other box just as Costain led Mrs. Leonard to her seat. They were both smiling innocently. Cathy joined Gordon as the curtain rose.

"What happened? Where did they go?" she demanded.

"He took her down to the lobby for a breath of air. I managed to overhear that much. She said she was feeling faint. I crept downstairs behind them,

97

but it was impossible to go to the lobby without being seen. There was no one there but the fellow who takes the tickets and a couple of post boys. We shall follow them home, of course."

"What can happen? Mr. Leonard is with them."

"Then we'll follow Costain."

Cathy had no objection to this idea. The play seemed to last a very long time. Her head was splitting long before it was over. What occupied her mind was what she should do now that she was convinced Lord Costain had turned traitor to his country. Obviously someone in authority must be told. The logical person to tell was his superior, Lord Cosgrave. She sensed that Cosgrave already mistrusted Costain, so he would listen to her.

Tomorrow she and Gordon must go to the Horse Guards and seek an interview with Lord Cosgrave. The interview loomed before her with all the horror of a trip to the tooth drawer. How could Costain do such a thing? He was an officer and a nobleman. What had he to gain by betraying his country? It was all *her* fault. The beautiful Mrs. Leonard had led him astray. He must love her very much.

Cathy did not feel up to any more sleuthing that night. She could not believe that Costain would attempt anything when the lady's husband was of the party. "You follow them, Gordon. I have a headache."

"How the devil can I follow them if I have to take you home? Perhaps Edison . . ."

"I cannot like to ask him. If we left now, you could take me home and be back on time to follow Costain."

"Yes, by Jove. I have lost all track of the play anyhow, so I shall have to come back another time. Grab your wrapper, then, and let us go."

Gordon whispered a word in Edison's ear and he and Cathy left the theater. When they reached King Charles Street, Gordon said, "If you want to learn what happened, wait in the study. We can talk there without disturbing anyone."

"Yes, I should like to hear what happens." Since she knew sleep would be impossible, the study was as good a place to wait as any.

Lady Lyman had just retired when Cathy reached home. Cathy was relieved to be spared putting on a smile and pretending she had had an enjoyable evening. She went to the study and lit the fire that was laid for the morning, then poured a glass of sherry and sipped it while gazing into the grate. The leaping flames did not warm her. She felt cold and empty inside. Costain was a traitor, and it was her duty to report him. She had no idea how long it might be before Gordon came home, but as it would probably be over an hour, she curled up in a padded chair and tried to get comfortable.

She had fallen into a lovely daydream when the tap came at the study door. Gordon had decided to enter this way. She rose and hurried to let him in. When she opened the door, Lord Costain stepped in, uninvited.

"Miss Lyman, I know it is late, but may I have a moment of your time?"

Chapter Ten

Cathy just stared, incapable of speech. She was not so much frightened as momentarily stunned beyond any sensation.

Costain watched as her lips trembled and her eyes, wide with fear, blinked nervously. "What an idiot I am! I've frightened you half to death. I am sorry, Miss Lyman. It is only your faithful old lion, Leo," he said, smiling to ease her fears. His gloved hands reached out and gripped her wrists to steady her. "You'll catch your death here. Let us close the door," he said, and placing an arm around her shoulder, he drew her into the study.

She twitched away. "What are you doing here?" she demanded. Her voice, though breathless, sounded truculent.

"There is no need to bite my head off. I didn't come to steal your books," he replied in an injured tone. "When I saw your light on, I thought perhaps you expected me. I noticed you noticing me at the theater." A smile grew on his handsome face as he removed his coat and tossed it aside, sure of his welcome. He walked toward the grate and held his hands out to the fire. "Ah, that feels good."

"I thought it was you in that box," Cathy said. When she took a seat on the sofa, he joined her. She was unsure how to behave, but soon decided to act as normally as possible. He thought a smile and a flirtatious word was all it took to con her. Let him think it! His conceit might serve her well.

"Those were the Leonards I was with," he said. "You would have recognized the fair Helena. The old fellow is Harold."

She nodded. "So I assumed. Who was the elderly lady?"

Costain stretched his long legs toward the blazing grate and drew a sigh of satisfaction. "A neighbor and relation, a Mrs. Newhart. Are you not curious to learn how I came to be with Helena?"

"I was wondering why you were with the Leonards," she said, not stressing the plural, but using it intentionally.

He cocked a brow and said brashly, "Point taken. Harold was there, too, though he is eminently forgettable."

"I noticed you forgot to include him at the intermission."

"Oh, that was intentional. I am not *that* forgetful. But we are beginning in media res here. Let me begin at the beginning. I decided to follow Gordon's lead and keep an eye on Mrs. Leonard this evening," he explained. "That is why I did not call on you. I followed the Leonards to the Royal Coburg and went in behind them, hoping to add myself to their party. The boxes were sold out, and when Mr. Leonard saw me turned away, he offered me a spare seat in his box. Naturally I jumped at the chance."

"Naturally."

"A demon for work, you see," he said modestly, but there was a dash of amusement in his manner. "At the intermission Mrs. Leonard said she felt faint." His eyebrows lifted in a manner that invited her to share his doubt of the claim. "And I, being a perfect gentleman, offered to take her out for a breath of air."

"Is Mr. Leonard not a perfect gentleman, that he might tend to his own wife's needs?"

"Certainly he is, but he is a gentleman of a certain age, and a certain physical infirmity. It is not only ladies who are plagued by advancing years. He offered to accompany her, but his wife expressed a great concern for his health. Well, to get to the cream of the story, I took Mrs. Leonard down to the lobby and propped the door open to give her the needed air without quite freezing the poor lady—and poor me."

"It is strange she left her wrapper behind."

"You used those glasses to good effect! Or did Gordon tell you? If he usually follows Mrs. Leonard as clumsily as he followed us tonight, I fear it can be no secret to her that she has picked up a shadow. I shall tell Gordon to stop dogging her."

Cathy didn't answer the question. "Did you learn anything of interest?" she asked.

"Mrs. Leonard is harmless," he said, waving a graceful hand in dismissal of the idea.

"And are her long visits to Mademoiselle Dutroit's establishment also harmless? She must have a great love of bonnets."

"Doesn't every lady? *She* certainly has, and she also possesses great skill in devising them. She works for Mam'selle Dutroit, to make a little money to eke out Leonard's earnings."

Something in his manner annoyed Cathy. Perhaps it was his smile of admiration when he spoke of Mrs. Leonard. "How did you learn all this during half an intermission, milord?"

"I can be a close questioner." He laughed. "It is not only you ladies who excel at gossiping. We got to chatting of this and that. Mrs. Leonard has had a hard life. She was married once before. Mr. Fotherington left her unprovided for. She was working as a milliner when she met Mr. Leonard at a small

102

private party of mutual friends. He was a widower, she a widow, both lonely and both in straitened circumstances. One sees how it might have come about. I believe it is a marriage of convenience, but with genuine love on his side, and what our elders call 'esteem' on hers.''

"I would have thought such an Incomparable could have done better than Mr. Leonard."

"One would think so indeed, but then, she went about very little. I sensed some irregularity in the first husband's demise, though she did not actually say so. Perhaps it was nothing more than a load of debt. That will always cast a cloud on the widow's social acceptability. And whom would she meet, working in a shop? Ladies, for the most part. It has not been my experience that ladies are likely to lend a helping hand to a woman more beautiful than themselves."

"On behalf of the less beautiful ladies, I must object to that cynical remark, sir. To say nothing of comparisons being odious."

"Present company is always excepted, ma'am," he said with a gallant bow. Cathy gave him a gimlet glance. "That lowered brow tells me I have inadvertently offended you. Naturally your beauty takes second place to none."

The compliment was a poor one, and its mundane delivery did nothing to redeem it. Cathy decided the best course was to ignore it. "So you think Mrs. Leonard is too beautiful to be involved?" she said blandly.

"Now, that, Miss Lyman, was downright nasty. I am shocked at your sharp tongue. It is not Mrs. Leonard's beauty but her story that convinces she is innocent. The only thing I could accuse her of is a slightly forward manner, and that would be a case of the pot calling the kettle black, so I shan't suggest that she might be open to a carte blanche, if the right gent made an offer."

"And did you?" she asked.

"No, Miss Lyman, I did not. Morality aside, it is poor policy to mix business and pleasure, and I work with the lady's husband."

Cathy poured her caller a glass of sherry, to give herself time to think. Costain could be telling the truth. She must not allow jealousy of Mrs. Leonard to color her judgment. If he were lying, he had gotten up a credible story that covered all angles in very short order and related it fluently, with no air of guilt or even apology. She decided to suspend judgment until she had had time to think, and discuss it with Gordon.

She passed him the glass of sherry. "So you think Mrs. Leonard is innocent?" she said.

"She is a bit of a twister, not much inhibited by virtue, but no worse than most ladies." He took a sip of his drink, then asked, "Where is Gordon?"

"He went on somewhere after the play."

"Ah, I thought when I saw your light in here that the two of you might be waiting for me to come and explain myself. You have some explaining to do as well, Miss Lyman. What of those letters you were going to write this evening?"

"I decided to go out instead."

"That denotes a sad unsteadiness of character," he said, shaking a playful finger at her. "I expected more firmness of character from you."

"Another case of the pot calling the kettle black?"

"No, gray. I am convinced you only delayed the writing till a later time. Which of the many gentlemen in your box lured you from your correspondence? Was it the blond fellow you rescued from falling over the railing? I must congratulate you on your quick rescue, and on your patience in the face of gross provocation. Had my escort been so inattentive, I would have given her a nudge over that railing."

"Mr. Edison is only a friend."

"Still, one expects a little consideration from

one's friends. Why, he is the sort of fellow who would abandon his lady at supper. But then, that would be nothing new for you. Did you read him a lecture, as you did me?"

"Actually he is Gordon's friend."

"I wondered why he paid so much attention to Miss Stanfield when he had a more charming lady by his side."

"You know her?" Cathy asked.

"I see a comparison loses its odium when it goes in your favor! Elizabeth Stanfield is my first cousin. As there is more than a decade difference in our ages, we were never close. Since making her debut, she has turned into a devout flirt. I fear the chit has lost what little propriety she ever had. And who am I to be preaching propriety when I come barging in on a solitary lady at this hour of night? I must go." He set his glass aside and rose to put on his hat and coat. "You will tell Gordon to stop following Mrs. Leonard?" he said.

Costain's easy manner had nearly convinced Cathy he was innocent. She had second thoughts when he repeated that Gordon must cease watching Mrs. Leonard. Perhaps he intended to accept the lady's hints that she was available as a mistress? Or perhaps she already occupied that position. That, while horrid, really had nothing to do with the spy at the Horse Guards.

"I shall tell him what you said," she replied.

Costain had put on his coat and was doing it up. He looked up, surprised at the ambiguity of her reply. Then he walked toward her. "What is the matter?" he said simply. Without waiting for a reply, he added, "You don't believe me."

"You could be telling the truth," she admitted.

"I *am* telling the truth. What possible reason could I have for dissembling?"

"I did not accuse you of dissembling."

"But you don't believe me."

Desperate for a reply that would satisfy him, she

said, "Perhaps it was Mrs. Leonard who was dissembling."

Costain's arched brows rose, and he tilted his head to one side to think. "That is possible. I would not be the first man to be led astray by a beautiful lady. I wonder . . ."

"Just so you bear the possibility in mind, milord," she said, and led him to the door.

"About tomorrow evening," he said, and paused, his hand on the doorknob. He had not intended to continue seeing so much of Miss Lyman. Yet her distrust bothered him in a way he could not quite fathom. He found he wanted her good opinion. He also realized he had taken an unaccountable aversion to that blond fellow who sat beside her in the box.

She watched him, not with the adoring eyes of an infatuated lady, but with something akin to dislike. "Perhaps you and Mr. Edison have already made plans. It is presumptuous of me to assume you are at my beck and call," he said with a question in his voice.

"I don't know—I cannot recall just offhand what we are doing tomorrow evening. Perhaps—"

"May I drop by after work?"

"Yes, I shall tell Gordon you will be coming."

"And *you* will be here?"

She looked at him with her wide, clear gaze. As he watched, a small smile crept over her face. "I shall probably be here, too," she said.

"I was telling the truth, you know."

"I know," she heard herself say. She had no idea where that soft voice, or those words, had come from. They rose up instinctively from the unconscious depths within her. She felt at that moment that he was telling the truth. It was impossible that he was not.

His frown lightened, then a smile seized his lips. He looked as if he might say something further.

But he just put on his hat and went to the door. "Good night, Miss Lyman," he said as he left.

"Good night." When he had disappeared into the shadows, she quietly closed the door.

A warm glow suffused her as she sat by the fire, waiting for Gordon to return. She felt some new height had been reached in her relationship with Costain. He wanted her good opinion, and why should he care about that unless he liked her? She did not let herself think the word *love*. He had not done or said anything to give that impression, but he had seemed to be aware of her as a woman in a way he had not before.

It was not long before Gordon came in, frowning and complaining. "I lost Leo. He just disappeared after the play. He did not get into the carriage with the Leonards, for I decided I might as well follow them home since I had lost Costain, and he was not in their carriage. I waited an age to see if Mrs. Leonard slipped out after the old boy took to his tick, but she did not."

"Lord Costain came here," Cathy said. "He explained all about his being with Mrs. Leonard." She went over the story carefully, excluding only those few flirtatious comments that she hugged to herself like a precious secret.

"And you believed him!" Gordon exclaimed derisively when the tale was told.

"Yes, I am sure he was telling the truth. His explanation covered everything we were concerned about."

"It didn't cover the carriage that was waiting at the back door of Dutroit's shop, and the man who drove Mrs. Leonard away. It wasn't her husband, for he was at his office. Why, for all we know, it was Costain himself. We have only his word for where he spent his day."

"You said it was a large, bulky man."

"Why, I could hardly even see that it *was* a man,

107

with those curst spectacles." He took a glass of sherry before continuing.

"If she has a rich gent at her beck and call, why would she be wasting her time making bonnets? His story has more holes than a beggar's coat. And if he was following the Leonards at a distance, how does it come they saw him, and offered him a seat in their box?"

"It seemed feasible, the way he told it," Cathy said, but as Gordon poked and pulled at it, the story seemed to fall to pieces before her very eyes.

"Why, it was nothing but a Cheltenham tragedy. I ain't sure I didn't see it acted on the stage a year ago. Something very like it, in any case. Costain takes us for a pair of flats, but he is out in his calculation. I know how many beans make five, whatever about you. He made up to you, and you let him sweet-talk you into believing that farrago of nonsense. I knew by the soft smile you had on when I came in that something had happened. I feared Edison had gotten at you in the carriage."

"Don't be absurd, Gordon. You know he is crazed for Miss Stanfield. Oh, did I mention she is Costain's first cousin?"

"The devil you say!"

"Yes, he mentioned it."

Gordon's scowl dwindled to a smirk. "How did he come to do that? Was she asking Costain about me?"

"No, actually he was taunting me about Edison paying so much attention to her. Somehow or other it came up that she is his first cousin."

"Wouldn't you know it! My first chance at an in with her, and I have gone and insulted Costain."

"What did you do?" Cathy demanded. "What did you say to him? I thought you had not followed him."

Gordon looked surprised, then a smile appeared. "I didn't actually say anything to him, thank God. It is just what I said to you, but he need not know

I think him a liar and a scoundrel until after he has puffed me up a little to Miss Stanfield. I mean to say, what do we actually have against him? It is plain as a pikestaff he is Mrs. Leonard's lover, having me follow her to see who else she has on the string, as you said. Nothing in that. It has nothing to do with the spy. An affair of the heart, nothing more."

This hardly satisfied Cathy, but as she was the perpetrator of the idea, she could not scold Gordon as she wanted to. "What do you think we should do?"

"The thing to do, we set up an outing with Costain and his cousin. You and Costain, me and Miss Stanfield."

"I mean about our work, Gordon."

"Oh, that! I shall keep hounding Mrs. Leonard, certainly. She would not have another lover when she has Costain sewn up tight as a drum. Stands to reason, the fellow she meets over the hat shop is the spy. Who else could he be? I shall follow him, find out who he is, and turn him over to Cosgrave. That will secure me a position on his staff. A pity about Italy, but I shan't forget to find you a parti. You might nail Swinton if you look sharp. He says you ain't as old as he thought."

Cathy honed in on the important of his speech. "You think Costain innocent, then?"

"Of course he is. A bit deluded, poor fellow, blinded by love, but down as a nail."

"How did he come to overlook the man who met Mrs. Leonard at the back door of the shop, though?"

"He didn't overlook him. He thinks it is a competitor for the fair Leonard, and was ashamed for you to know he is carrying on with the trollop."

"Oh, do you think that is the explanation?" she asked in a small voice.

"As plain as the tail on a fox. Well, this was a pretty good night's work. Miss Stanfield's first cousin, eh? Thank God for it, or he would cut us all out. I can hardly wait to see Edison's ugly phiz when I tell him I am stepping out with Miss Stanfield."

They extinguished the lamps and went quietly upstairs, to avoid awaking the household. Gordon slept the sleep of the innocent, but Cathy found her mind in such confusion that she was awake for hours, trying to make sense of it all. She came to the conclusion that Lord Costain was either Mrs. Leonard's lover, or a very stupid spy. She could not feel that he was stupid. Deeply engrossed in her brooding, she even forgot that tomorrow evening was the date of the Great Winter Ball.

Chapter Eleven

"Did you enjoy your evening at the theater?" was the first question Lady Lyman put to Cathy when her daughter entered the breakfast parlor the next morning.

"Very nice, Mama."

A glance at Cathy's wan face was enough to tell her that the chit had not had enough sleep. As she had heard her daughter mount the stairs to bed at midnight, she could only conclude that the girl had slept poorly. A long career of reading ladies' hearts and minds from their faces suggested that her daughter's romance had come a cropper. This, in turn, suggested that Lord Costain had been at the theater with another lady.

"Did you happen to see Lord Costain?" she asked.

"He was there with another party," Cathy replied, feigning indifference.

Lady Lyman was too kind to humiliate her daughter by inquiring whether this party had included a young lady. She knew from her career as a diplomat's wife that when a contract between parties was in danger of souring, a new initiative was called for. The Lymans were no longer the courted party; it was for them to take the initiative. Cathy had been pestering her to go to the Great Winter Ball. It was shockingly dear, but to hang such an ornament as Lord Costain on the family tree was well worth fifty pounds.

She cleared her throat preparatory to making her announcement, and when she had her audience's attention, she said, "Lady Eagleton coerced me into buying tickets for Lady Somerset's charity ball last evening—what they are calling the Great Winter Ball, though I doubt it will merit the title. I thought I might drop Lord Costain a line and ask if he is free to take you to it, Cathy. It is to be held this evening."

"This evening?" Cathy exclaimed. How had it crept up on her so quickly? She had been ticking the days off on her calendar, but once Costain entered her life, she had forgotten even the Great Winter Ball.

"My dear, you cannot have forgotten? You badgered the life out of me."

"Oh, no, Mama! You must not ask Costain," Cathy said.

Costain's new lady must be pretty! "A pity to waste the tickets," Lady Lyman complained. She was sorry she had claimed to have purchased them already.

Gordon came into the breakfast parlor, tugging at a cravat of monumental proportions.

"Good God, what is that thing at your throat?" Rodney demanded.

"It is called a cravat, Uncle," Gordon said with heavy sarcasm. "The Oriental, to be precise. All the gentlemen are sporting it this season."

Rodney shook his head. "It will soon go out of style, like damped muslin. You ought not to be a galley slave to fashion. You make yourself ridiculous."

"Ridiculous, is it? I'll have you know, Edison and

112

Swinton are sending their valets to see mine this very day, to learn how to tie this thing."

"Swinton is all sail and no anchor, like his father before him. Blown by every breeze of change."

"What's that to do with me?" Gordon demanded. "I ain't the one following fashion. I set it."

"If you wish folks to think highly of you, you ought not to speak so highly of yourself."

Gordon passed his cup for coffee and let the matter drop. Silly old fool, what did Rodney know of fashion? He was still wearing black jackets. It was enough to make a cat laugh, him giving sartorial advice. "Did I hear you say you had bought tickets for the Great Ball, Mama? You must have won the lottery."

Lady Lyman had hastily pondered the situation and come up with an alternative for throwing Cathy in Costain's path. "I hope I always do my bit for the less fortunate. Gordon, are you free to accompany Cathy this evening? It is to be a stunning party, to judge by the price of the tickets."

"I will not take my sister to a ball, and that's final." Gordon scowled. What would Miss Stanfield think, to see him sunk to stepping out with his sister?

"Then I shall take you myself, Cathy," Lady Lyman said.

Gordon smirked into his cravat. "Will you stand up with her, too, Mama, to announce to the world that she cannot nab a beau?"

After a prolonged squabble, no conclusion was reached, and the conversation turned to different matters. But Cathy felt a pronounced desire to attend that ball, preferably with a dashing gentleman.

"I am happy to see you keeping decent hours, Gordon," Lady Lyman said as she tapped the shell of her coddled egg. "What will you be studying today?"

"Irregular verbs," Gordon replied readily. He had

been studying these mischievous articles for some weeks, when the mood took him.

"I thought you must know them by now." She turned to Rodney. "How is he doing? Is he making any progress at all?"

"Have you finished that translation for my perusal, Gordon?" Rodney inquired. "Or have you been too busy arranging your cravat?"

"Nearly finished, Uncle," Gordon lied. "I shall have it ready for your red pencil in jig time." He cast an appealing eye at Cathy, and she jumped in to assist him.

"Did you learn anything about Mrs. Leonard last night, Mama?" she asked.

"Yes, I meant to tell you, but my poor brain, you know, is full of holes. She was a Helena Johnson, who married one of the Fotheringtons, an M.P. The poor fellow was riddled with debt, and put a pistol to his head, leaving the gel destitute."

As this jibed with what Mrs. Leonard had told Costain, Cathy had to believe it. "How did she survive after his death?"

"She had to work. I believe she had some skill as a milliner, and turned to that trade. No one seemed to know how she had met Mr. Leonard."

"Fotherington, I recall him," Rodney said, scraping his empty eggshell for a stray crumb. "The fellow was never any good. A gambler and a knave."

"There was a scandal about gambling debts," Lady Lyman said. "It seems he may have been selling state secrets at Amiens, during the peace talks."

Gordon's head jerked up. He exchanged a wild look with Cathy. "What's that you say, Mama? A traitor, was she?"

"Not Mrs. Leonard, Gordon. Her husband, Fotherington. Helena—that was her name—was well liked. No blame attached to her."

"I see," Gordon said, swallowing a smirk of disbelief. He rose from the table, leaving his eggs untouched. "Well, time to get at those irregular verbs. Don't you have something to translate this morning as well, Cathy?"

"Not today, but I shall work on Uncle's copy." She rose, and the pair of them nipped off to the study to discuss their latest discovery.

Lady Lyman directed a gimlet glance at her brother. "She has lost out on Lord Costain. We must do something to buck up her spirits, Rodney."

"I'll take her to the ball myself if you think it will help."

"I shall buy the tickets from Lady Eagleton and go with you. I might achieve some rapproachement with Costain yet. Such a suitable parti. I fear this disappointment might send Cathy into a decline. She cannot afford that at her age."

"Marriage is overestimated," Rodney said.

"Marriage is delightful. It is the trials of widowhood that are underestimated. Although, I must say, Gordon is improving. He used to fret and complain at having nothing to do, but nowadays he is studying from morning till evening. I wonder if I should bother with my Christmas rout."

Rodney, seeing his nephew's untouched eggs, reached out and helped himself to them.

In the study, Gordon paced and pounced about the room in a state of high excitement. "A traitor, by Jove."

"Mama said it was Mr. Fotherington who was the traitor, Gordon," Cathy pointed out.

"At his wife's instigation, no doubt."

"It would be best to watch Mrs. Leonard a little longer and see what she is up to. Watch her like a hawk, Gordon."

"You need have no fear of that. I have smuggled a footman's outfit into the cupboard. I must wiggle into it before Uncle comes."

"Mama will keep him gossiping for ages. Breakfast is her favorite time for reminiscing. About the Great Ball, Gordon, do you not think you and I might go together? It is a shame to waste the tickets."

"They an't wasted. The ball is for a good cause—charity, I think it is."

Gordon nipped into his uncle's office before Cathy could talk him into the ball. He emerged moments later in the bottle green of the Lymans' livery, with a dashing half cape over his shoulders for warmth. "I shall be back to meet Leo at five," he said, cocking the footman's tricorne hat at a rakish angle over his eye.

"Come sooner if you learn anything," Cathy said urgently. "I am on nettles with all the responsibility of this affair."

"My dear girl, stop frowning, or you'll destroy what is left of your face with wrinkles. I shall handle this. No one expects a lady to do anything."

Gordon opened the study door, peered up and down the street to see he was unobserved, and skulked off in the direction of Half Moon Street. The weather had warmed sufficiently to melt the snow which now ran in rivulets along the gutter. He was glad the curst wind was taking a rest.

It was clear as glass to Cathy that Gordon was enjoying himself immensely. It was all a game to him, but for her the excitement had turned to dismay. No matter which way she slanted events, she could not return Lord Costain to his former eminence. How had he fooled her so completely the night before? She went over their meeting a dozen times, but to return Costain to his former integrity was like trying to put Humpty Dumpty together again.

After long consideration she decided he was Mrs. Leonard's dupe. In that manner she could pity him instead of despise him, but she could not esteem him. He had poked fun at the word, but without esteem there could be no love.

Chapter Twelve

Cathy worked desultorily on Rodney's copy that morning. At eleven a client came with a letter written in French in a wavering hand on sere, yellowing paper. He wished to have it translated. The owner, Mr. Culpepper, had the air of a provincial—a solicitor or doctor perhaps—to judge by his modest toilette.

"I found it in the family Bible," he explained. "My ancestors were French, but we have lost the language over the years. We hope it may establish a link with a certain noble house in France," he said proudly.

Cathy studied it with interest. "It uses very old French," she explained. "The date, you see, is 1649. I shall have to do a little research to make sure the translation is accurate. Can you leave it with me?"

"Certainly, but I hope you can get at it right away. I am in from Devon, and hope to return at first light tomorrow."

"I shall do my best, sir. Come back this afternoon."

The translating helped to divert her thoughts. She feared Mr. Culpepper would be disappointed.

The letter was a nagging one to a neighbor, threatening to take him to court over a cow. Nothing in it suggested the writer was an aristocrat, though he must have been a gentleman, as writing was the preserve of the upper classes at that time.

At lunch Lady Lyman mentioned that Gordon had asked for a tray to be taken to his room to avoid interrupting his studies. Cathy assumed that Gordon had taken his valet into his confidence. She wondered where her brother really was at that hour. Was he even now watching as Costain paid a quick noon-hour visit to his lover?

The food lodged in her throat, making every bite a struggle. When an apple tart appeared for dessert, she rose and excused herself.

"I am not very hungry, Mama. Mr. Culpepper may arrive while I am out. I shall go back to the study now."

"We ought to have a sign at the door, directing clients to the front door if they get no answer," Rodney said.

This was an old argument with Lady Lyman. "I will not have every Tom, Dick, and Harry coming to my front door, Rodney. You may direct them to the back door if you wish. I have no objection to that."

"You cannot expect clients to deal with a cook!" Rodney pointed out.

Cathy slipped away while the familiar words echoed behind her. She was surprised to hear a sound at the street door as she entered the study. She had not expected Mr. Culpepper quite so soon, and wondered if Uncle Rodney actually was missing clients by having no notice at the door. She hurried forward, for the knocking was loud and insistent, as if it had been going forth for some moments.

She looked at the young man who was seeking entrance. She had met him only once, but she recognized him immediately.

"Mr. Burack!" she exclaimed. The idea popped

into her head that something awful had happened to Lord Costain. He had been discovered. "What is it?" she asked in a hushed voice.

"May I come in for a moment, Miss Lyman? I am sorry to disturb you at lunchtime, but it is rather urgent, and this is the only time I could get away."

She moved aside and he came in, peering over his shoulder to see if he was watched. He removed his curled beaver, but he did not take a seat, and in her confusion Cathy did not offer one. She remained standing, too.

"Are we alone?" he asked in a low voice.

"Yes, for the moment. What is it? Why have you come? Is it Lord Costain?" The questions burst out in a rush.

"Exactly. I am relieved you already suspect something of his doings."

Her hands flew to her heart. "What has he done?" she asked in a whisper.

"I don't know, for certain. I have some reason to suspect, however, that he is using his position to discover our war plans—for what purpose you may imagine."

Cathy's mouth was dry. She swallowed wordlessly, encouraging Burack by her strained interest.

"He obtained a highly secret document that he had no right to see, and worse, he removed it from the office. He returned it, but we don't know that he had not made a copy, or what he may have done with the copy."

"When was this?" she asked.

"Four days ago. It was quite by chance that I discovered it. The clerk asked me if Lord Cosgrave had received a certain letter. I knew he had not, for he had been in meeting for some time. I asked the clerk where he had put the letter. He said he had handed it to Lord Costain. Costain had left the building. The letter certainly went with him, for I searched his office and Lord Cosgrave's and Mr. Leonard's thoroughly."

It was the letter Costain had brought to her that they were discussing, then. "Why are you telling me this?" Cathy asked. Burack didn't know Costain had brought it to her! She might yet protect Costain if she said nothing.

"I have often noticed the sign on your door. The letter was in German. Costain does not speak German. As you are his friend, I thought you might have helped him—not realizing he had no right to the letter, of course," he added hastily, and with apparent sincerity. "I do not mean to accuse you of any wrongdoing, Miss Lyman."

"Does Lord Cosgrave know of this?" Cathy asked, to play for time while making her decision.

"Certainly, it was his idea that I come to you."

Lord Cosgrave knew, so there was no point in trying to hide it. "I did translate a letter for Lord Costain," she said. "He thought it might be urgent, and wished a translation in a hurry."

"Then why did he not take it to Lord Cosgrave, who reads and writes German fluently?"

"He does?" Cathy exclaimed. It was like an arrow piercing her heart. Costain had not told her that. His excuse was that he did not trust the translators, but he must certainly trust Lord Cosgrave.

"Certainly. Has Costain asked you to translate any other letters?"

"No, only the one."

"I take it he pledged you to secrecy?"

"Yes." And she had broken her promise to him.

"Does he call often? Is he keeping you in good humor, to ensure your assistance at a future date if it should be necessary?"

Her reply was a whisper. "Yes."

"Excellent!" Cathy looked at him as if he were mad. "If what we suspect is true," Burack continued, "then he will bring you more letters. You must let us know at once. If we can catch him redhanded, he will not be able to deny it."

"How can I inform you?"

"Say you are having difficulty—you must keep the letter and send word to the Horse Guards at once."

"But if it is only a short note, as it was before, he will suspect if I claim I cannot translate it."

"That's true," Burack said, nodding. "I'll ask Lord Cosgrave to have him followed if he leaves the building. You can do a translation—mislead him with false information. When he leaves, he will be followed and apprehended. I would appreciate it if you would still notify me the instant Costain leaves you. He won't have gotten far. I should like to be there to haul him in myself. To think he would use his position to betray his country," he said, shaking his head in disgust.

"I cannot believe he would do it, Mr. Burack. He is an officer. He fought for his country. He would not have to do it for money. He is wealthy."

"His weakness is women," Burack said sadly. "Some lady has gotten at him, no doubt."

The name Mrs. Leonard hovered on Cathy's lips, but she withheld it. "Have you any idea who she might be?"

"She might be anyone. He goes about a good deal in society."

"Perhaps Mrs. Leonard?" she suggested, watching him closely.

Mr. Burack stared. "Mrs. Leonard? Surely you are joking."

"No, indeed. I think she may be the one leading him astray."

"Why would she need Costain? Mr. Leonard is privy to more secrets than his lordship, and he is very obviously enamored of his wife. He speaks highly of her."

"But that is not to say he would betray his country."

Burack gave a dismissing shrug. "I cannot believe Mrs. Leonard is involved. You saw Costain with her last night at the Royal Coburg?"

"Yes."

"I was there myself. I have been following Costain about since he took that letter. I have not discovered the lady's identity yet, but common sense suggests she is surely a Frenchwoman. I shall continue looking into his social life."

"You'll let me know?" Cathy asked. When Burack looked surprised, she felt a little foolish. He must wonder why she was taking such a personal interest in all this.

"I will not be at liberty to divulge my findings until the matter is settled, Miss Lyman. We are all under a strict code of secrecy at this sensitive time, as I am sure you realize. After it is over, I will tell you the whole story if you wish."

"Thank you."

Mr. Burack stood a moment, just looking at her. "The devil of it is that I do not have the entrée to such places as his lordship goes in the evening. Who knows what passes behind drawing room doors?"

Cathy remembered her mother's tickets for Lady Somerset's ball. She had felt the odium of not having a beau to escort her. Here was a more than presentable gentleman who was eager to enter society.

"Will you be attending Lady Somerset's ball this evening?" she asked in a strained voice she hardly recognized as her own.

"Not I. The tickets cost more than a month's wage."

"I have a spare ticket. That is, Mama bought a pair. I had thought I might attend . . ."

A blaze of joy lit Burack's rather fine eyes. "I say! Are you hinting that I might accompany you?"

"Yes."

A shadow passed over his face. "Costain will think it odd that I am with you."

"We met the other evening," she reminded him. "It is none of Lord Costain's concern if you have called on me since. In fact, you asked if you might."

"So I did, and you were kind enough to give me permission, but I have not been able to get away at work. About the ball, I shouldn't like to tip Costain the clue I am checking up on him," he said uncertainly.

To her astonishment, Cathy found it possible to flirt with a gentleman so long as she had no real feelings for him. She adopted a moue and said, "Why should he think anything of the sort? I go about with several different gentlemen."

"I noticed, at the theater. Very well, we'll do it. I shall call for you at half past eight. I don't know how to begin thanking you, ma'am. I did not expect this degree of cooperation."

Mr. Burack looked much more handsome when he smiled. He also looked younger. He thanked her a couple of times, then said, "I must be going. I need not pledge you to secrecy. Naturally you will do what is proper in that respect. The safety of England depends on it, Miss Lyman."

"Of course," she murmured.

Mr. Burack bowed and left. When he was gone, Cathy found herself comparing his behavior to Costain's. There was no denying Mr. Burack behaved more properly. Costain paid no heed to secrecy. Now that she knew even Lord Cosgrave suspected him, she found a dozen flaws in his behavior.

Removing the letter, and asking a woman he had never seen before to translate it should have tipped her the clue he was doing something wrong. And all his calls, his friendliness and flirtation—Burack had hit it on the head. Costain was keeping her in humor to oblige him with another translation done on the sly, should the need arise. She had been used, but she would have her revenge.

With her help, milord Costain and his French mistress would be caught yet. How had she and

Gordon been drawn into suspecting Mrs. Leonard? Naturally she would not need Costain, when her own husband had a more important position at the Horse Guards. Costain had set Gordon to watching her to lead them astray. It seemed the beautiful Helena was not his mistress after all. He had directed suspicion on an innocent lady to protect his real mistress. Was there no limit to the man's treachery?

Then she remembered that he was calling on her that very afternoon. In two hours he would be knocking at her door, and she would have to smile and dissemble, and pretend to be happy to see him. Cathy did not often resort to tears, but she felt she was about to do so then, and fled up to her room in case Rodney should return to his office.

Chapter Thirteen

As Cathy sat brooding over her translation that afternoon, it was not the obscurities of Mr. Schiller's philosophy that absorbed her, but Lord Costain's perfidy. As four o'clock drew near, her uncle Rodney's usual time for departure, another trouble was added to her load. Rodney did not leave, but settled in with a pipe to repine once again over Schiller's being led from the path of philosophy by Goethe, to write what the undiscerning masses called the best plays in the German language. He prosed on for a quarter of an hour.

"A great pity, but there you are. Drama's gain is philosophy's loss. A charismatic character like Goethe or our own Lord Byron can do such a deal of mischief in the world. You always want to watch out for anyone who tries to lead you from the path of duty, Cathy. Not that anyone is likely to in your case," he added when she cast a woebegone look at him.

"Is it not time for your tea, Uncle?" she said.

"You run along. I shall stay behind to give Mr. Culpepper his letter. I shall have a cup of tea brought in here and continue with my work, for it is going uncommonly well today."

"I believe I smelled Cook's scones," she tempted him.

"Is that so? Hot scones, eh? Well, perhaps I can spare half an hour from my work. One must feed the body as well as the mind."

Cathy was confident he would not return. Like Schiller, he was easily tempted from the path of duty. Mr. Culpepper arrived at four-thirty and read the translation of his letter with no pleasure, until Cathy pointed out that reading and writing were quite an accomplishment in the seventeenth century.

"That is true," he said, leaping on it like a hound on a hare. "He was obviously of the gentry—no saying he was not an aristocrat."

He was much inclined to remain behind and discuss it, but eventually she got him out the door. It was ten to five. Cathy spent the interval until Costain's arrival in trying to calm herself. Burack had stressed that she must behave as naturally as possible, but how could she greet a traitor with friendliness?

At five o'clock Gordon arrived, shivering and claiming that his king and country had best reward him with a medal, for a wicked wind had sprung up from nowhere, and he was suffering worse than the soldiers in Spain. "At least they do their work under the sun. I am frozen to the marrow. We must design warmer coats for our footmen. It is monstrous for them to have to stand around in the icy weather in these little capes." He went to the gate to rub his fingers into life.

"They do not usually have to stand around all day in the cold" was all she said before rushing into the tale of Mr. Burack's call.

"Burack, eh?" Gordon said, narrowing his eyes. "No doubt Cosgrave put him up to it."

"He did. How did you guess?"

"Guess?" he exclaimed, offended. "It was no

126

guess. I have discovered Mrs. Leonard's lover. It is none other than Lord Cosgrave himself. He would not want a decent-looking fellow like Costain sniffing around her. He is out to sabotage Costain's career. Cosgrave called on Mrs. Leonard this afternoon."

"Lord Cosgrave! You must be mistaken, Gordon."

"Devil a bit of it. I'd know his porky carcass anywhere, even if he was bundled up to his ears, with his curled beaver tilted over his eye. If he weren't so fat, I'd say he was your intruder. He fears discovery, you see, and has set on Leo as the scapegoat. This explains why he had to use a hansom cab t'other day at Dutroit's. His own carriage has a lozenge on the panel."

"But in case Costain is guilty, Gordon, we must not tell him of Burack's visit, or Cosgrave's suspicions."

"It is my feeling that Costain is as innocent as a babe. I must report to him that Cosgrave was with Mrs. Leonard. This is a major development. The villainy goes straight to the top. Can you doubt the fine hand of the Duke of York is in this somewhere? Remember the Mrs. Clarke affair? We all know what *he* is, letting his *chère amie* sell commissions in the army."

"What has that to do with Lord Cosgrave?" she asked.

"Money, my girl. There is money in selling state secrets as well as commissions. Cosgrave and York are as thick as thieves."

"Well, but we need not tell Costain the rest— about Burack's visit," Cathy said after a hasty consideration of this new twist in affairs.

"Leave it up to me," Gordon said, swelling up his chest and looking important, just as his father used to do.

While Cathy was still struggling to assimilate the situation, the knocker sounded, and Lord Costain entered. In confusion, she remembered Uncle Rodney's warning of charismatic men, and Mr. Burack's order to behave naturally. *Can this man be guilty of treason?* she asked herself. She knew at least that he could sway her from the path of duty.

It was Costain's carefree manner that firmed her resolve to behave naturally. If he could enter smiling and complimenting her on her gown, she could act her part, too.

"Any interesting callers today?" he asked, wondering why she stared at him as if he were a scarecrow. Why was she acting so unnaturally? The sherry sat on the table. He wondered that she did not offer it.

She rattled on nervously about Mr. Culpepper's letter, hoping that Gordon would not mention her other caller. Gordon's clenched face alerted her that he was scheming deeply.

"Anything new at the Horse Guards?" Gordon asked, his eyes narrowed to slits in an effort to behave naturally.

"Business as usual. Lord Cosgrave left early, but no interesting missiles arrived after his departure."

"P'raps you would like to know where Cosgrave went," Gordon said. Excitement gleamed from the slits of his eyes.

"You spotted him?" Costain inquired with no excess of interest.

"Hard to miss him when he went right to Mrs. Leonard's front door, carrying a folder with him, and left half an hour later, empty-handed. She did not leave the house all day, and had very few callers. Only Lord Cosgrave, early in the afternoon, and shortly after he left, Mademoiselle Dutroit arrived, carrying a hat box. She stayed close to an hour. Clear to the meanest intelligence she carried away a copy of the papers Cosgrave gave Mrs. Leonard in that same box."

Costain's brows arched in mild interest. "Mr.

Leonard was home sick today. A touch of gout. I expect Cosgrave took him some work to do."

"When he was sick?" Gordon asked, disbelieving.

"He was not bedridden. Sore toes prevent a man's walking; he can still read and write." He gazed into the grate awhile, then said musingly, "Mr. Leonard is quite often home sick. If Cosgrave is in the habit of taking, or sending, work to him, then it would be possible for a clever wife to get a glimpse of it, I daresay."

"There you are, then," Gordon said, happy to have Miss Stanfield's cousin free of taint without slandering Lord Cosgrave. They were both innocent, and it was Mrs. Leonard alone who was the culprit. "Told you it was a bag of moonshine, Cathy."

She cast a damping frown on her brother, who emitted a high-pitched laugh and said, "Pay no heed to my sister's scowls, Costain. I never suspected you for a moment."

Costain's dark eyes turned slowly to Cathy. "Suspected me of what, pray?" She felt as if his eyes were boring a hole through her brain.

"Nothing," she said, but the pink flush creeping up her neck belied the word.

"Come now, a lady does not blush so prettily at nothing. You and Gordon had decided I was Mrs. Leonard's mentor?"

"Certainly not," Cathy said, her flush deepening.

"We only thought you were her dupe," Gordon assured him. "And you need not look daggers at us, Costain, for it was Burack put the notion in Cathy's head with his visit."

"He did not!" Cathy objected. But it was too late to hide that Burack had indeed called. "He was sure Mrs. Leonard had nothing to do with it," she added.

"You never told *me* that," Gordon pointed out.

"We had only a minute to discuss it before Lord Costain arrived. Mr. Burack was nonplussed at the very idea."

"How did he pick up on Mrs. Leonard—that is what I should like to know," Gordon said.

"I may have mentioned her," Cathy said vaguely.

"Why would you do an addle-pated thing like that?"

She avoided looking at Costain when she replied. "He mentioned Costain's weakness was ladies."

Costain listened with an air of derision, his eyes turning from one to the other as the argument proceeded, as if he were watching a badly played game of battledore and shuttlecock.

Cathy became aware of his searching gaze, and sat up, primly tidying her gown. "He especially asked us not to say anything to Lord Costain," she reminded Gordon.

Costain cleared his throat, preparatory to speaking. "What else had my colleague to say of me?" he asked.

"Nothing! That's all," Cathy said, and shut her lips firmly.

"He just dropped in to say that he suspected me of treason, and gave no reason?"

"He asked me the other evening at Lady Martin's if he might call," Cathy said.

"But surely he meant call on you in your mama's saloon," Costain pointed out.

"The reason he came here was the letter you brought for Cathy to translate," Gordon replied.

"And pray how did Mr. Burack know that if you did not tell him, Miss Lyman?"

"I didn't tell him!"

"Then he already knew. He discovered I had taken that letter, and guessed that I had darted to the closest translator—you. And you were kind enough to confirm his suspicions."

"I didn't, at first ... I told him you would not do such a thing. That is when he told me of your weakness for—er, ladies," she said, gazing out the window into the denuded branches of an elm tree.

"I wonder where Mr. Burack gets his misinformation. We do not travel in the same social circles," Costain said haughtily.

"There is no point cutting up stiff with Cathy," Gordon said. "She is only a lady. We never should have dragged her into it in the first place. The way it looks to me, Burack is picking up a certain aroma. Why was he so swift to defend Mrs. Leonard when it is plain as day she is in it up to her eyebrows, whatever about anyone else?"

"A good question, Sir Gordon," Costain said. "Why indeed, unless to limit your suspicions to myself?"

"That was precisely my meaning. He is using you as a red herring over the trail. I begin to think it is Burack I ought to be keeping my peepers on. Did you happen to notice his thumbs, Cathy?"

"No, I didn't."

"You may just be right about Burack," Costain said quietly.

Remembering her date with him that evening, Cathy stared in consternation.

Gordon nodded his agreement. "And of course Mrs. Leonard is in it. I mean to say—all that fishy business at Amiens."

"Amiens?" Costain asked. His arched brows nearly disappeared into his hairline.

"Didn't we tell you? She has been a spy forever, reaching back to the Peace of Amiens, in 1802, or whenever the deuce it was signed. Naturally I kept following her when I learned that."

"Certain people suspect that Mr. Fotherington was spying, but even that is only a rumor," Cathy pointed out.

"No smoke without fire," Gordon insisted. "Why did he aim that pistol at his tonsils? Tell me that!"

"Perhaps one of you will be good enough to tell me this tale from the beginning, starting with this Mr. Fotherington," Costain said, and eventually he had the gist of it from their bickering.

131

He turned to Cathy. "I assume you did not inform your friend Burack of this, Miss Lyman?"

"The matter did not come up, except that when I mentioned Mrs. Leonard as a possible suspect, he wouldn't hear of it. He felt, you see, that your lady friend must be French."

This began to strike her as highly suspicious behavior on Burack's part, almost as if he knew Mrs. Leonard was guilty and was protecting her.

"If Helena was in France during the peace of Amiens, then one assumes she has some French friends," Costain said musingly.

"She has nothing *but* French friends, if you want my opinion," Gordon declared. "There is Dutroit, and Mrs. Marchand, the modiste, and I am not sure by a long shot that Whitfield hasn't a French look about him."

Costain said, "Mrs. Leonard and Burack, perhaps . . ."

"Cathy said Burack's pockets are to let," Gordon informed him. "He can scarcely manage to make buckle and tongue meet. He is in it for the blunt, like Mrs. Leonard, and trying to shift the crime onto you."

Cathy listened, an image of Burack at the back of her mind. She did not think Burack had lied to her. He had seemed very sober and sincere, with his demand for secrecy, and his warning that the welfare of England was in her hands. That struck her as the proper behavior, and not this carefree carrying-on of Costain's.

"What should I do tomorrow, Leo?" Gordon asked eagerly. "Burack will be at work all day. There is no point loitering in front of the Horse Guards. Shall I keep watch on Mrs. Leonard again?"

"That might be best."

"I shall dart up and change before Mama sees me. I must devise a new disguise for tomorrow. I froze my tail in this dashed getup. Don't leave until

I return. We have to decide on tonight's surveillance."

He left, and Costain turned to Cathy with a cynical smile on his lips and fire in his eyes.

Chapter Fourteen

Cathy played with the folds of her skirt, determined not to be intimidated by Costain's manner. She watched as his tight smile dwindled to a sneer.

"Had Burack anything else to accuse me of?" he asked stiffly.

"No, you were not the sole subject of our conversation," she replied.

"I wonder what he will make of this visit? I assume he is having me watched."

"He will think you are keeping me in spirits, in case you require another quick translating job, perhaps," she suggested, and looked closely for his response.

Costain rose from the sofa and began pacing. His brows drew together. "You sound as if he is innocent! Can't you see what he is up to? He is trying to discredit me. His first visit may have been vague and tentative, a warning only, speaking of 'other things,' to beguile you into friendship. Next time he will ask your help. Don't be surprised if he wants you to notify him of what I have had translated."

"Is there likely to be a next time, milord?" she asked archly. Excitement lent a sparkle to her eyes and a breathless tone to her voice. She could not decide which of the men was innocent. It was beginning to seem that she must play them both along, and eventually make her own decision.

"Why don't we devise one?" he suggested. "I have a footman deliver a letter to me at the Guards, I slip out of the office and fly to you. I write a message up in English, which you put into German. Let Burack have a copy, it can do no harm, for it will not contain any real information."

"What is the point of that?"

"I follow him and see where he goes with it."

"But he will be following you."

"He will if he is innocent. If he takes the message elsewhere—well, it would be interesting to see what he does with it, *n'est-ce pas?*"

"You think he might take it to Mrs. Leonard?"

"Or even a milliner or modiste," Costain replied.

Cathy tried to weigh the criminality of fooling Mr. Burack if Costain was the culprit. Would she end up in the Tower? On the other hand, if Burack was the bad spy, it was imperative that he be stopped. She had often wished for some excitement in her life when she sat in this very room translating Mr. Schiller's philosophy. She had not thought it would be so very difficult and confusing. Her only wish now was that she had never met either Lord Costain or Mr. Burack.

Costain watched as her inner turmoil played itself out on her face. "What harm can it do?" he asked. "If Burack is innocent, I should be happy for his assistance. With two pairs of eyes at the Guards, we might achieve more success. I shan't rush you into anything, however. Let us wait and see if Mr. Burack asks you to notify him of any further messages."

"Very well," she said in a small voice. Her decision seemed to have made itself. She would not tell Costain the request had already been made, but she would leave the door open to test Burack, since she could see no harm to England in it. It would be a spurious message, so even if Burack got to his French colleagues, nothing would be revealed.

Costain gave her a deprecatory look. "I sense a fading of your eagerness for this business, Miss Lyman."

"On the contrary. I am as eager as ever to help my country."

"Don't let your eagerness lead you into danger. If you receive an urgent message from Burack asking you to meet him in some out-of-the-way spot, don't go."

"What would he want with me? I am no danger to him."

"No, but if he suspects that I am on to him, you would make a fine bargaining tool. He believes that you and I are old friends. I am speaking of abduction," he said bluntly when she frowned in confusion.

Her eyes widened in fear as she remembered she was going out with Burack that very evening. "I did not mean to frighten you, but it is best for you to be aware of possible danger," he said more gently.

"But—" She stopped, unsure whether she should reveal her outing with Burack. "You must warn Gordon, too," she said.

"I shall, but they are more likely to abduct a lady. There is some special urgency in knowing a helpless lady is in danger, vulnerable to the violence of men without a consciense."

"Costain! You are scaring me to death!"

He reached across the sofa and seized her hands in a firm grip. "Good. That is precisely what I want to do. Don't take any chances—with Burack or anyone else. It would be my fault if anything happened to you." As their eyes locked, he felt himself being drawn deeper into her gaze, until he felt he was drowning. Was he mad to have involved an innocent young lady in this dangerous business? If any-

136

thing happened to her— He swallowed and said, "I am the one who involved you in all this. It was not my intention, you know."

Cathy gently withdrew from his grip. The warmth of his fingers lingered, making her hands tingle. She felt that Costain was behaving more as a proper spy and an eligible gentleman ought, with his warning and his hand-holding.

"It's not your fault," she allowed graciously. "If we had not followed you to St. James's Park, we would not be so deeply in it as we are."

"The fault is mine. I should not have come to you in the first place. You need not continue to be involved. In fact, there is no reason I cannot take my spurious letter to someone else for translation. There must be dozens of independent translators in London. I shall find someone else—"

"No!" The word came out loud and clear. "No," she said more calmly. "It is not often that a lady has the chance to be involved in important affairs. If I can help, then I should like to do so."

His admiring smile was reward enough. "Pluck to the backbone, Miss Lyman." His fingers came up and just brushed her cheek. "But you will be careful," he said softly. "I don't want anything to happen to you."

Although acutely aware of the message in his soft stroke, she replied only to his words. "Of course I shall." Her lips opened to tell him of her date with Burack that evening, then she closed them. "When will you bring the new letter for translation?"

"Not for a few days. I shall need a little time to look into the private lives of Burack and Mrs. Leonard." He drew a weary sigh before continuing. "It will go hard with Harold if his wife is involved. His sun rises and sets on her."

Gordon returned, outfitted for the evening in black jacket and pantaloons. "Have you decided what we are to do tonight, Leo?" he asked.

"Actually, my name is Daniel," Costain said. His eyes turned to Cathy.

He did not ask her to call him Daniel, but she felt there was some personal message there, some warmer look than she was accustomed to.

"Yes," Gordon said, "but for business, you know, it is best to throw any stray listener off guard, so I refer to you as Leo."

"I am flattered that you think me the king of the jungle. And what a jungle it is in these perilous times. About this evening, Lady Somerset is having a large charity ball. We might all go there." He looked hopefully to Cathy. Her heart shriveled in regret. "Lady Cosgrave is one of the hostesses. Cosgrave sold me tickets last week. I shouldn't be surprised if he also sold them to Burack and Leonard."

Again Cathy opened her lips, but before she could speak, Gordon said, "Leonard cannot go when he has the gout."

"That is not to say Mrs. Leonard will not attend," Costain said. "We shall all go. I have half a dozen tickets. It was for a good cause. I meant to give Liz Stanfield a few of them."

Gordon looked as if he had been struck by lightning. "Miss Stanfield! She might as well go with our party," he said when he had recovered the use of his wits. "Mean to say, it is a bit late for her to get up a party of her own."

"I shall stop by now and see if she is interested."

"Remind her it is for a good cause," Gordon said. "*Make* her come."

"No one makes Liz do anything, but I expect she will come. She was bemoaning last evening that the winter was a dead bore." He looked at Cathy and said, "I shall call for you—"

She finally got her speech out. "Actually, I am attending the ball with—with Mr. Burack," she said, and felt unaccountably foolish.

"*What!*" Costain stared in disbelief.

138

"I am attending the ball with Mr. Burack," she repeated.

"Are you mad? When did this happen? Why did you not tell me?"

"It was arranged this afternoon, when he called."

"Haven't I just been telling you to stay away from him? Gordon, tell her this is insane."

"You would have a much better time with us," Gordon said.

"You can't go alone with him. It isn't safe," Costain said, and began pacing the floor.

"But if I withdraw the invitation—well, it will look so very odd, and rude," Cathy said, but she was hoping to be overborne.

"That is true," Costain said over his shoulder. "Gordon, you'll have to go with her."

"I'll do no such a thing. I shall go with Miss Stanfield."

"I have spare tickets. Ask your mama or uncle to accompany you," Costain said, turning back to Cathy.

Gordon leapt on this solution. "Mama was planning to go anyhow, was she not, Cathy? When I refused to take you, she said she would use the other ticket and go with you yourself."

Costain's anger rose a notch higher at this revelation. When he spoke, his voice was thin. "Am I to understand you are standing buff for the evening, Miss Lyman? I can only assume that you also did the inviting. I fear you must have omitted the more interesting bits from your description of Burack's visit."

Gordon emitted a loud guffaw. "By Jove, I would give a monkey to have seen Cathy screwing up her courage to ask a fellow out. That will go into your diary, I wager."

Costain reached into his pocket and handed Cathy two tickets. "Promise me you won't go alone with Burack."

She read the anger in his eyes, and, beneath it,

something that looked strangely like genuine concern. Perhaps even a tinge of jealousy . . .

"Very well," she said, and took the tickets.

"What time is he calling for you?" Costain asked in a tightly controlled voice.

"At eight-thirty."

Costain said to Gordon, "I shall be here at eight. We'll pick up Liz and be back here by eight-thirty."

"What the devil for?" Gordon asked in confusion.

"To see that your sister is not abducted," Costain said, choosing the hardest words he could find.

"You are being extremely foolish," Cathy said mildly. But inside, a warm mist of pleasure swelled. Costain was jealous—of her and Mr. Burack.

Costain rose to begin his leave-taking. "You will be ready at eight sharp, Gordon? I shall drop by the Stanfields now and tell Liz that if she is not punctual, we shall go on without her."

Gordon stared to hear anyone speak so firmly of Miss Stanfield. "I am ready already," he replied.

Costain made a curt, angry bow. "Until this evening, then," he said, and walked quickly to the door to let himself out.

In the study, Gordon shook his head. "Pity you invited that mawworm of a Burack to the party. How did you come to do such a thing? Costain did not like it above half."

"It is none of Lord Costain's business," she replied with an angry *tsk*, but in truth she bitterly regretted her rashness. She might have gone to the ball on Lord Costain's arm.

"Whatever you do, don't ruin my chances with Miss Stanfield, Cathy. You know I have been dangling after her forever. This is my big chance."

He darted back upstairs to improve his toilette without waiting for assurance.

As Costain leapt into his waiting carriage, he knew his anger was out of all proportion to Miss Lyman's offence. She had no reason to suspect Burack of anything when she invited him to the ball.

She was free to do as she pleased, but the angry thought would not be kept down. Why had she not invited *him,* if she had tickets? Other girls were constantly inviting him to parties. Cathy's mama made no secret that she approved of him, so that was not the problem. No, the simple fact was that she preferred Mr. Burack to himself. He had given her a disgust of him with his overbearing manner.

And as a result she was going out this evening with a man whom he half suspected was a spy. It seemed more than likely Burack was the infamous masked intruder. It was Burack who had followed him to King Charles Street. How else could he have known that the Lymans were involved? He would want close watching tonight.

Chapter Fifteen

"What is that horrid smell?" Lady Lyman demanded as Sir Gordon, reeking of Steak's Lavender Water and wearing another extravagantly arranged cravat, took his seat at the dinner table. "I trust you have not dowsed yourself in scent, Gordon. A gentleman has no need of scent."

"Just a dab behind my ears," Gordon replied. "All the crack, Mama. You are a million years behind the times. Everyone uses it nowadays."

"In my day, scent was for ladies," Rodney announced.

"This is the nineteenth century, Uncle," Gordon replied.

"I did not notice Lord Costain wearing scent," Lady Lyman said with a smile in her daughter's direction. "So kind of him to give Cathy his extra tickets, even when she refused to accompany him to the ball. Very clever of you, my dear, inviting Mr. Burack. That made Lord Costain open up his eyes and look sharp. There is nothing like a little competition to hasten a match along."

A dish of turbot in white sauce was passed to the dame, and she helped herself to a fillet. For once, a pleasant meal was enjoyed at King Charles Street. Lady Lyman was pleased with her offspring. Cathy looked pretty in that deep blue moiré gown. The dark color and severe cut added a touch of sophistication. Nothing was so aging as mutton dressed as lamb.

She was aware that she looked elegant herself in a gown of gentle mauve that was kind to her fading complexion. It would be pleasant to have an evening out with old friends. This do would refresh her memories of how a proper evening party was held. The Christmas rout was back on track.

It was the main subject of conversation over dinner. Gordon was assigned the task of hiring musicians. Lady Lyman expressed no interest whatsoever in Mr. Burack. He was but a means to an end. When he arrived at eight, she saw that he looked like a gentleman. That was enough to win him a smile.

Lady Lyman and Mr. Reynolds accompanied Burack and Cathy, which inhibited any private conversation between the young couple. Cathy was minutely aware that the carriage dogging their tail held Lord Costain's party. When the two carriages unloaded in front of the stately mansion on Curzon Street, Lady Lyman spotted Costain and latched onto his arm for the trip up the stairs, thanking him effusively for the tickets.

She had mentally settled on the twentieth for her rout. That would give Costain time to be in touch with his mama about inviting Cathy to Northland with him for Christmas. "I have a little rout party planned for the week before Christmas. I hope you can join us, Lord Costain," she said.

"I would be charmed, ma'am," he replied without even asking the date. His attention and his eyes closely followed Cathy and Burack's progress to the front door. Lady Lyman considered him as good as won.

A fluttering excitement invaded Cathy as she was

143

announced at the ball. She was here! She had made it to the Great Ball. Behind her shoulder Lord Costain hovered, quite taking the shine out of the gentleman at her elbow. She gazed below at the elegant guests, the ladies all sparkling with diamonds and the gentlemen hovering attendance like a swarm of uxorious penguins. The hall was decorated with fir boughs and red and gold ribbons encircling the pillars. An enormous fir tree stood in one corner. Cotton wool arranged amid the branches gave the appearance of snow, and small gilt boxes dangled from the boughs. Perhaps they contained trinkets for the ladies.

Cathy's eyes followed Costain as they all descended to the ballroom. Gilt letters a foot high were strung across the doorway, spelling out HAPPY CHRISTMAS.

"Who is the chit he is standing up with?" Lady Lyman said.

"Miss Stanfield, Mama, the girl Gordon likes."

Miss Stanfield, unaware that her duty was to fall in love with Sir Gordon, chose her cousin as her first partner.

"A common-looking chit," Lady Lyman decreed, her gimlet eyes assessing the Incomparable. "When one sees an excess of garniture on the gown, one knows one is looking at a commoner. She does not require sequins and lace *and* bows." A veteran now of her first Season, Miss Stanfield wore a powder-blue gown festooned with a plethora of all three. "And a flirt into the bargain. See how she is rolling her eyes at the bachelors."

"She is Lord Costain's first cousin," Cathy said.

This close kinship removed Miss Stanfield as possible competition, and added greatly to her charms. "Uncommonly pretty," Lady Lyman decided. "I notice a greater use of decoration in the gowns these days. You might want to tack a few bows onto your skirt, Cathy."

Cathy went to the floor on Mr. Burack's arm. As

144

they performed the intricate steps of the opening minuet, she found it hard to transmogrify her partner into a dangerous spy. He was shy and admiring. She sensed that his stiffer demeanor that afternoon was the result of duty overcoming shyness.

"It was kind of you to invite me, Miss Lyman," he said two or three times. "Your mama, too, was very nice. Not so toplofty as I feared."

She was suddenly struck with the fact that Mr. Burack was quite a young gentleman. "Have you been at the Horse Guards long, Mr. Burack?" she asked.

"Only a few months, since graduating from Oxford."

Good gracious! He was not much older than Gordon. It was ludicrous to think him a hardened villain. "You haven't made any more discoveries at your office?" she asked, to remind him why they were at this ball together, since he seemed to have forgotten.

"Nothing of any significance occurred this afternoon. I notice Mrs. Leonard has just arrived," he said, glancing to the doorway, where she had entered with her elderly companion. "Her husband is at home with the gout."

Cathy turned to examine Mrs. Leonard. The lady had gone to a deal of trouble to enhance her natural beauty. She looked striking and dramatic in a gown of shot silk, with diamonds at her ivory throat. The gown looked black at first glance, but as she moved, flashes of deep burgundy appeared. Before she had gone two paces into the room, a gentleman accosted her.

"She is very attractive," Cathy said.

"Do you think so? For an elderly woman, perhaps. The lady with her is handsome. I wonder who she can be?"

"The younger lady is Mrs. Leonard, Mr. Burack," Cathy said, surprised that he didn't know it.

"You mean to tell me that dasher is married to old Leonard? Good Lord! No wonder he is always boasting of her. I thought the old pelter must be his wife. She sat with him at the theater the other evening. Now I see why you thought Lord Costain might be her lover."

This pretty well convinced Cathy that Burack was too uninformed to be the spy. "Who is that man with her?" she asked.

"That is Mr. Fortescue, from the Horse Guards."

"Could he be her cohort?" Cathy asked. She was not happy to assign the role to either Costain or Burack. There must be someone else. "If she is a spy, I mean."

Burack said, "Fortescue is only a sort of financial liaison man with the government. His job is to try to get more money out of them, but he doesn't have the spending of it."

At the minuet's end, Lord Costain wished to dash up and snatch Cathy from Burack's arm. They were both smiling too much to suit him. He knew his duty was to deliver Liz Stanfield to Gordon, however. Before he could do it, Gordon appeared at his elbow in the company of someone called Miss Swanson.

"Our dance, I think, Miss Stanfield?" Gordon said, and took her arm. Costain, perforce, had to smile and ask Miss Swanson for the next set.

Neither Lady Lyman nor her daughter was pleased with it, but as an extremely eligible earl asked to be presented to Cathy, they overcame their chagrin. At the end of the second set, Costain directed one scowl on Cathy before crossing the room and asking Mrs. Leonard to stand up with him. At the termination of that set, Cathy returned to her mother, who had deprived herself of the pleasures of the card parlor to oversee her daughter's progress and offer such hints as her vast experience of a world long past suggested to her.

"I could swear that is Helena Fotherington with

Costain!" Lady Lyman said. "You recall you were asking about her just the other day, Cathy. She has not changed one iota. How on earth does she do it? I must say good evening to her. That will give Costain the chance to stand up with you. Come along, Cathy."

Cathy suffered the exquisite embarrassment of hounding off after Costain and hearing herself described to the beautiful Mrs. Leonard as "my little girl, Cathy. All grown up now."

Mrs. Leonard smiled dutifully. "I have already met your daughter, Lady Lyman," she said, but her questioning gaze did not suggest the slightest memory of the mother.

"We met in France, at Amiens," Lady Lyman said, to jog her memory. "You may recall my late husband, Sir Aubrey Lyman?"

"Certainly. I was sorry to hear he had passed away. And do you have any other children, Lady Lyman?"

"One son, Gordon. He is here somewhere."

"Ah, you are fortunate. I have no children, just my little pug dog. He is keeping my husband company this evening. Harold is a martyr to gout. He would insist I come, as Lady Cosgrave is one of the hostesses. We spent the entire afternoon here, Lady Cosgrave and I, overseeing preparations. I scarcely had time to run home and have a bite of dinner and change." As she spoke, Mrs. Leonard's infamous eyes toured the room, seeking her next escort.

Before long she had caught the attention of a well-known rake, and was carried away.

"Miss Lyman, may I have the honor of the next dance?" Costain asked.

As no squares were forming, Cathy knew the waltzes were about to begin. She felt a nervous shiver when Costain drew her into his arms.

"What did you think of that?" he asked with a meaningful look. "Mrs. Leonard spent the entire afternoon here, if we are to believe her. Did Harold

147

entertain Mam'selle an hour by himself? And how did Gordon miss seeing Helena leave the house?"

"I expect he nipped around the corner for lunch, and that must be when she came here—if she did come here."

"I don't see why she would lie about it," he said.

Cathy just shrugged, and said Mam'selle Dutroit had probably taken tea with the servants. That would account for her lengthy visit. He noticed Cathy's spirits had been more animated when she was with Burack. "Mr. Burack will be sorry to miss out on waltzing with you," he said in a rather stiff voice.

"He is very nice. I don't think he can be the spy after all."

"You are easily convinced! Mrs. Leonard is also 'nice,' whatever that means. Does her niceness exonerate her from any blame?"

"Mr. Burack didn't even recognize her. He thought the companion was Mrs. Leonard."

"Is that what he told you? Interesting," Costain said.

"Why, are you saying he *did* know her before?"

"I don't know," Costain admitted, feeling foolish. "But he might have."

"Did she say anything of interest?" Cathy asked. She sensed Costain's animosity and felt an anger rising in herself to meet it.

"No."

"Perhaps that is not why you were in such a rush to stand up with her? She's uncommonly pretty."

"I hope I am not so green as to believe a pretty face is any sign of innocence. Did Burack say anything of interest?"

"He's been at the Horse Guards only a few months. Just down from Oxford—how could he be involved? It would take time to establish the necessary contacts."

This was not how Costain wanted to spend his few private moments with Cathy. He had been

148

looking forward to being alone with her, to getting to know her better, and here he was, behaving like an unlicked cub.

"Perhaps you're right," he agreed. After a moment's silence he spoke in a friendlier tone. "Your mama has invited me to a rout next week."

"Will you come?" she asked with an air of utmost indifference.

"Certainly I shall. I look forward to it. I'll bring Liz if you like. That is my cousin, Miss Stanfield."

"I know."

Cathy's indifference acted as a goad to Costain. Something had changed her, and he soon fingered Burack as the culprit. It was impossible to hold a meaningful conversation with the music and the commotion all around them.

"Let us go to the refreshment parlor," he said. Without waiting for her reply, he waltzed her from the floor.

At the doorway into the ballroom they met Gordon, scowling and sulking. "I hope you are discovering some interesting secrets, Costain," he said. "Otherwise this evening is a dead loss."

"You have stood up with Miss Stanfield," Cathy reminded him.

"Yes, for a dashed country dance. A fellow cannot make any headway there. She refused to give me the waltzes."

"She could not stand up with you twice, Gordon," Cathy pointed out. "You hardly know her."

"She didn't have to accept Edison's offer, did she? Look at him, grinning and smirking."

They looked to the dance floor, where Edison was sharing his smirks evenly with Miss Stanfield and Gordon.

"I've a good mind to land him a facer," Gordon declared angrily.

"Come to the refreshment parlor with us and have a glass of wine instead," Costain suggested.

"We shall discuss the case. There has been a new twist," he added as further enticement.

"What is there to discuss? I have checked out Cosgrave's thumbs. He ain't the intruder, though he is certainly carrying on with Mrs. Leonard. I saw the pair of them whispering behind the potted palms. Women!" he said with a cynical *tsk*. "I am going out for a breath of air. If Miss Stanfield happens to notice I am missing, you might say I stepped out to blow a cloud. Not that she'll care." And not that he smoked cigars, for that matter, but he thought it rather a dashing thing to do.

He turned toward the exit. "Put on your coat, Gordon. You'll catch your death of cold," Cathy called.

"Good!" he said, and marched out the door.

"It must be something in the air," Costain said with a bantering smile. "This evening is not conducive to successful romancing."

"If you would like to join Gordon . . ."

"That was not my meaning, Miss Lyman," he said. With a firm grip on her arm he led her into the refreshment parlor.

Chapter Sixteen

Curzon Street was alive with carriages. "Poor, deluded creatures," Gordon muttered to himself as he watched the eager faces of the latecomers hastening on to Vanity Fair. They looked forward to an innocent evening's pleasure at the Great Winter Ball, but e'er cock's crow, there would be a dozen hearts smashed to bits, like his own. Maidens would be seduced by fortune hunters, wives lured to betray their husbands, homes torn asunder. Love was a cruel mistress.

He was enjoying a mood of dark despair, and disliked to have to interrupt it so often to nod or speak to acquaintances. When a school chum asked him if Miss Stanfield was at the ball, Gordon could take no more.

He said, "I believe you'll find her waltzing with Edison," and strode away from the house of doom.

The wind snatched at his coattails as he walked briskly along the darkened street. A small object appeared in his path, and he kicked it. It was a stone, not a frozen apple as he thought, and it inflicted severe damage on his toes. Now he ached at both extremities.

If Miss Stanfield wanted to spend her time with that jackanapes of an Edison, that was her loss. She'd realize her mistake when she read of Sir Gordon Lyman's death of pneumonia. In his mind it was no less than a state funeral, complete with black-plumed horses and a cortège, that he envisaged. Somehow the world would discover how he, single-handedly, had foiled the French menace and made England safe for women and children.

When he got to the corner, he decided to go back to the ball. Leo had mentioned some new twist to the case. Mean to say, no point catching pneumonia until the case was solved. He realized he was at the crossing with Half Moon Street, just half a block from Leonard's house. He'd take a stroll past and see if there were any comings or goings. Not very likely, with Mrs. Leonard at the ball, but if he spotted Dutroit slipping in, it would be interesting.

He did his spying from the far side of the street. Not really expecting to see anything, he was surprised when the front door opened. An old man let Mrs. Leonard's dog out to do its business. Nasty little beast it was, yapping its head off. The dog headed right for him, of course, giving away that he was watching the house. Gordon continued along, as if he were just passing. The curst mutt kept following him, nipping at his ankles, and he didn't have his boots on either, to protect him.

"Come back, May," the old man called. Was he Mr. Leonard? He looked like him, but all old men look alike at a glance.

Gordon kept walking. Before he knew what he was about, the old man came dashing down the stairs, calling the dog. A carriage was bowling along, causing some fear that the dog would be run over.

"Stop her, lad!" the man called. Gordon ran forth and rescued the mutt from the approaching wheels.

The fellow in the carriage let down his window and called, "When was you appointed dog catcher,

Lyman?" Graham Grant, wouldn't you know it? The story would be all over town.

"Here you go," he said, handing the beast to its master.

"It is my wife's dog. I wouldn't want anything to happen to it. Nice, doggie. Come along."

His wife's dog. Then this man *was* Mr. Leonard. The dog made a nip at Leonard's fingers. Leonard released it with a little howl of pain, and it took off after Grant's carriage, bent on suicide, with Mr. Leonard in pursuit. He did not move as quickly as a younger man, but he moved with suspicious alacrity for a gentleman who was supposed to be gout-ridden. There was something havey-cavey here.

Leonard looked over his shoulder, breathing heavily. "Can you catch her? She is too quick for me," he gasped.

Gordon took to his heels after the mutt and lifted it into his arms. This caused such raucous amusement to Graham Grant that he had his carriage stopped to gawk and jeer.

The old man was still panting from the exertion. "Let me carry the dog for you," Gordon said, and they set out together for the familiar house on Half Moon Street. Mr. Leonard held on to Gordon's arm, for he was exhausted. But he was not limping. Gordon mulled this over as they walked along through the darkness. He might use this canine rescue as an excuse to get into the house and do some looking around.

At the doorway, Leonard said, "Thank you very kindly, Mr.—"

"Gordon. Mr. Gordon." That would throw him off the trail if he recognized the name Lyman.

Mr. Leonard smiled his thanks. "Can I offer you a glass of wine, Mr. Gordon? I fear you may have taken a chill. I see you are not dressed for the outdoors."

Gordon said, "Why, thankee, sir. I just stepped out for a moment from the Great Ball, around the corner, you know. I could do with a wet. It is thirsty work, chasing a dog."

He carried the dog into the house and Mr. Leonard took it. Gordon examined the entrance hall suspiciously. Neither the parquet floor nor the ornate mirror suggested nefarious doings.

"I'll just lock May up," Mr. Leonard said. "She is a bit noisy tonight. Let us go to my study."

Leonard seemed mighty shy of offering his name. Should have introduced himself. It would be interesting if he claimed to be someone else.

Mr. Leonard disappeared with the dog, and Gordon went into the study. After checking over his shoulder, he darted straight to Leonard's desk. There were letters sprawled all over its surface—letters to and from the Horse Guards. This would be the work Cosgrave had brought him to do at home. Gordon picked up one letter and glanced at it. He found himself staring at Beau Douro's signature. The man who was trouncing Boney's army in Spain, by God! He felt a tingling in his fingers, as if the force of the signer were running into his own body.

He glanced at the date, and could hardly believe it had arrived so quickly. Surely ships took longer than this? He turned it over, and saw a note that it had arrived by carrier pigeon. The letter did not convey much to Gordon. Something to do with moving troops over the Pyrenees. No doubt crucial, and here it was, not only let out of the Horse Guards, but actually hand-delivered to the house of a spy by the head of intelligence.

Gordon heard a sound at the door and jumped into the closest chair. He was just trying to look relaxed when Mr. Leonard came in, carrying a tray of wine. "Here we are," he said, setting it down on his desk and pouring two glasses.

"You got the dog settled down all right, did you?" Gordon said, adopting a conversational manner as he accepted the wine.

Mr. Leonard put his glass to his lips. "She's always restless when my wife is away. She is really my wife's dog."

Gordon happened to look at the glass, and noticed the stubby, spatulate fingers wrapped around it. His heart leapt into his throat. The last time he had seen those fingers, they had been pointing a pistol at him. He heard a sharp gasp, and realized through his confusion that it had come from himself. He swallowed, and struggled to control his excitement.

"I had a spaniel when I was a lad," he said in a high-pitched voice that bounced off the walls and echoed foolishly in the room. He cleared his throat and added, "Excellent sherry" before he had even taken a sip.

"Do try it," Mr. Leonard said, taking a sip of his own.

Gordon gulped down a mouthful. "The dog is giving you trouble, is she?" he asked, hoping to con Leonard into thinking he was harmless, but his brain was scuttling over plans to capture the enemy. Should he dart back to the ball and enlist Leo's help? He measured Leonard's shoulders, his age and infirmity, against his own youthful strength, and decided he could do the job alone.

"Dogs are a nuisance in the city."

Gordon tried to keep his eyes from returning so often to those stubby fingers, but as if his eyes had a mind of their own, they kept returning. He must look away, or Leonard would realize he'd been recognized in spite of having his face all muffled up the day he broke into the study. Something nagged at the back of Gordon's brain. What was it?

The stubby fingers began to blur from such strained viewing. Gordon shook his head to clear his vision. The thing to do, he'd pick up that brass paperweight and crack Leonard over the head with it as soon as the man turned around.

Old Leonard was prattling on with some pranks

of May's, something to do with getting into this office and eating a letter. An important message from the Peninsula, no doubt. Gordon sipped his sherry and nodded. He felt a mellowing ease wash through him. Miss Stanfield's face appeared in his head, smiling adoringly at his heroism in single-handedly capturing this vicious criminal. And still that something nagged vaguely. It suddenly came to him. Leonard's face had been covered that day he broke into the house, but his own had not. Why did Mr. Leonard not recognize him?

His glass was suddenly empty. The stubby fingers were proferring the bottle. "Why, thankee. P'raps another drop."

He watched the amber liquid enter his glass, and leave again as the glass tilted in his fingers. Damme, he'd smell like a tavern when he returned to the ball. He tried to straighten the glass, but it weighed a ton. Try as he might, he could not straighten it. The last thing he saw before keeling over was the crystal glass falling to the floor and bouncing. Within seconds his own inert body joined it on the floor.

There was a sudden influx of guests into the refreshment parlor when the waltzes ended.

"I am sorry Gordon's evening is such a disappointment to him," Costain said. "Let us have a word with Liz, to see the chit remembers she is to join our table for supper."

Cathy looked worried. "I wonder if Gordon has come in yet. He'll catch his death out in the cold without a proper coat."

"I'll have a word with the servants at the door."

They went into the lofty paneled entranceway together. Costain spoke to the man at the door.

"He never came back, sir. I'd begun to wonder about it. Still, he should be safe in this part of town."

Costain took the message to Cathy. "The idiot

has gone home to teach Miss Stanfield a lesson," she said.

"He asked us to remind her he would be back shortly."

"He wasn't wearing a coat, and he came in your carriage, so—ask if your carriage has been called for, Costain."

A different servant was in charge of guests' carriages. Costain made the inquiry, and returned to tell Cathy that the carriage hadn't been requested.

Cathy blinked in astonishment. "Where on earth could he be? He's been gone half an hour."

"I'd best scoot out and have a look for him."

"Don't forget your coat," Cathy said.

"Yes, Mama," Costain replied, not in a jeering way, but with a rather satisfied smile.

The doorman indicated the direction Gordon had taken. Costain hurried along, peering into shadows. He was more annoyed than concerned at Gordon's childish behavior.

As Cathy waited in the entrance hall, Mr. Edison came prancing up to her. "I say, I hope Gordon ain't sore with me. I've been looking all over for him."

"You haven't seen him?" Cathy asked.

"Not since the waltzes. Graham Grant mentioned he saw him chasing a dog on Half Moon Street." Cathy frowned. Gordon had spent a deal of time there recently, watching Leonard's house. No doubt he had decided to walk past and see what was afoot. "He was helping some old gaffer catch the mutt, I believe," Edison said. "Should have been back by now."

"I cannot imagine what happened to him."

"I'll send Grant along to have a word with you."

"Thank you, Mr. Edison."

Mr. Grant, another of Gordon's lanky young friends, appeared at Cathy's side five minutes later. "I hear you was asking for me, Miss Lyman?"

"You saw Gordon, Mr. Grant? Pray, tell me all about it."

"Not much to tell. I was just on my way to this do when I spotted Gordon chasing a yapping pug on Half Moon Street."

Mrs. Leonard had a pug, and an elderly husband who might be the old gaffer referred to. "A pug dog, you say?" she asked.

"It looked like it. I can tell you what house it came from, for the door was open, you know, and the light shining. It was the second house from the corner of Curzon Street. Gordon went to the house with the old fellow."

"Thank you," she said. "That's where he is, then. We have—friends living there." Whatever Gordon was up to, she had no desire to cause unnecessary commotion.

"Very happy to be of help, ma'am," Mr. Grant said, and dashed off to the refreshment parlor to quiz the ladies.

Cathy took a seat in the shelter of a potted palm and waited for Costain's return. She felt fairly sure now that Gordon had inveigled his way into Leonard's house to spy. But what was taking him so long? When Costain returned, she would ask his help. But could she trust him?

Costain remained away for a troublesome length of time. Long enough to rouse a fear that he, too, was going to remain away, spying, while the best ball of the whole winter went forth without him. It was more than a quarter of an hour before Costain returned, alone and wearing a worried frown. Cathy hurried forward to meet him.

"Has he come back?" Costain asked.

"No. You didn't see him?"

"I did a quick tour of the neighborhood. You realize we are within a stone's throw of Leonard's house?"

"Yes, and I have learned that Gordon was helping Leonard chase a small dog. One of Gordon's friends saw him and told me. He said Gordon went

158

to the house. Perhaps he went in. I'm afraid something has happened to him, Costain."

Her pale face was pinched with worry. Costain wanted to reassure her and said without thinking, "What could happen? Very likely Gordon was invited in for a glass of wine. He'd accept, to see what he could see."

"But he's been gone for ages."

Costain was worried, but he made little of it for her sake. "Don't worry. Leonard wouldn't recognize Gordon, and Gordon would hardly announce what he was doing there."

"If the intruder was there, *he* would recognize Gordon. But Gordon would not recognize him."

Costain could no longer feign indifference. "I'd best pay a call on Mr. Leonard," he said.

Chapter Seventeen

Cathy's first rush of gratitude soon ebbed to doubt. She must not put her whole faith in Costain; she had no proof he was entirely innocent.

"I shall go with you," she said, and immediately realized this was the worst thing she could do. With both Gordon and herself captured, there was no one to save them. Unless Burack . . .

"This is not lady's work," Costain replied firmly.

He appeared genuinely concerned. "You cannot go alone! If you fail to return, what can I do?" she asked.

Costain stood a moment with his brow furrowed. "If I am not back within fifteen minutes, tell Burack what has happened. And tell him to inform Castlereagh."

She felt easier in her mind at this suggestion. "Then you trust Mr. Burack?"

"It seems Leonard is our man. As you said, Burack is just down from Oxford."

Mr. Burack, who had been looking for Cathy, came rushing up to them. "Miss Lyman, I have been looking all over—" He stopped, glancing from

Cathy's frown to Costain's grave expression. "What has happened?" he demanded.

"Young Lyman's disappeared," Costain said. "He was seen at Leonard's house. We think he's being held there."

"Harold Leonard?" He looked a question at Cathy.

"You can trust Lord Costain," she said.

Burack appeared to accept it. He said to Costain, "Are you suggesting Leonard is the leak?"

"It looks like it. He was alone at the house all afternoon. His wife was here, helping the ladies prepare the ball. Lady Cosgrave confirmed it," he added aside to Cathy. "Cosgrave took some papers to Leonard. A French milliner called later, and remained a considerable time."

"One can scarcely believe it of Mr. Leonard," Burack objected. Then he said, much "Of course his wife is expensive, and we don't make money at the Horse Guards."

"You'd best grab a coat. It's cold out," Costain said.

"I'll be right back." He bowed and ran off after his coat.

Cathy remained behind in an agony of turmoil. Within a minute Burack was back, pulling on his coat as he ran toward them. "How do you plan to rescue Lyman?" he asked Costain.

"I've been conjuring with that problem. We must get him out safely before tackling Leonard. I believe our best bet is for me to walk up to the door and ask to speak to Gordon, say he was seen entering the house. That will tip Leonard the clue we know he is in there. He won't risk harming Lyman when he knows we know that. If I don't come out, notify Castlereagh."

"Very well. Let us hope he hasn't done the deed already."

Cathy's heart tightened in her chest. "Done the

deed already." He meant already murdered Gordon. "I'm going with you," she said.

Both gentlemen expostulated, but she stood firm. "You cannot stop me. He is *my* brother. I'm going, with you or by myself. You can both go to the door. I shall remain outside to notify Castlereagh if you don't come out."

"We cannot both go storming up to the door. It will look odd," Burack said, "as if it were an important office meeting or some such thing."

Costain's mobile brows lifted, and a tight smile appeared at the corner of his lips, but his eyes were hard. "Very well. Get your pelisse," he said to Cathy. "I shall call my carriage. You won't want to wait alone on the street."

Costain ordered his carriage and Cathy ran off for her pelisse, hardly able to believe he had agreed so readily.

"Now's our chance," Burack said, and headed for the door as soon as Cathy left.

Costain remained where he stood. "Wait," he said.

"We cannot take Miss Lyman. It could be dangerous."

"There is safety in numbers, Burack."

"Surely this is a matter for secrecy."

"Great secrecy. A matter of the utmost urgency has arisen, and Lord Cosgrave has called a meeting at Mr. Leonard's house for convenience, as Mr. Leonard is ill with the gout, and we are all so close at hand, here at Curzon Street."

"I don't see what you are getting at, Costain."

"Privacy, Burack, and security. The servants must all be sent to their rooms to avoid their overhearing the monumental secrets we shall be discussing. You and I, sent in advance, must ensure that the house is safe. That will require a search of the premises."

"For Lyman," Burack said with a reluctant grin.

162

"A bold plan, Costain. If you're wrong, it will cost you your job."

"Then it will be up to you to carry on at the Horse Guards. Did Castlereagh ask you to snoop on me?"

"Not you in particular. He asked me to keep my eyes open for any suspect dealings in the office. You behaved more suspiciously than anyone else, slipping that letter to Miss Lyman for translation."

"You followed me?"

"No, but I learned of the letter, and your leaving right after receiving it. As you were back so fast, I figured you had taken it to the closest translator, Mr. Rodney Reynolds. Why did you do it? Cosgrave reads German."

"And was drinking heavily that day."

"No unusual occurrence," Burack said with a sigh. "I mentioned the letter to Harold Leonard, by the bye. He came into the office shortly after you left. When Leonard went storming out, I thought he'd gone to pester Cosgrave. I wonder if he did not slip out of the building and follow you himself."

"It looks that way. If he'd mentioned it to Cosgrave, I would have heard about it. The only thing Cosgrave said to me was that I ought not to have taken the letter to Castlereagh. He didn't know I had had it translated."

"We ought to have been working together all the while," Burack said. "When you received that mysterious missile from Spain, I was sure I had found my spy."

"A note from an old army buddy."

Burack nodded. "About Miss Lyman—must she accompany us?"

"My groom was with me in Spain. She will be perfectly safe outside in the carriage. Ah, here is Miss Lyman now."

Mrs. Leonard watched their comings and goings from the corner of the refreshment room, that gave a view of the hall. She had been watching them for the past quarter of an hour, ever since receiving that unsettling note from Harold. So like him to make a muddle. Harold had assured her no one knew of young Lyman's visit, but obviously Costain had discovered it somehow.

She did not frown, for it left wrinkles on her aging skin. When she spoke to her companion, she touched her temples with her two fingers and gently massaged. "I hope you will pardon me. I have a touch of migraine."

She whisked upstairs for her cape and fled out the door without a word to her hostess.

Outside, Costain had escorted Cathy to his carriage. He entered with her and removed a pistol from the side pocket. Cathy just watched, fear written large on her face. "You will be careful, Lord Costain," she said in a hushed voice.

"Why, you are giving me the idea you care. I am flattered, ma'am." One hand came out and tilted her chin up. His face in the shadowy darkness was a pale blur punctuated by the gleam of his eyes. Costain lowered his face to hers and brushed a light kiss against her lips. It was as insubstantial and brief as the touch of a moth's wing, but it stirred her to the core.

"I have been wanting to do that for the longest time," he said, his lips at her ear. Then he lifted his head and said, "We shall discuss this interesting development in more detail after we rescue Gordon. Take care." His hand slid slowly down her throat, leaving a trail of heat in its wake. Then it was gone. Costain was gone, disappeared out the door, and the carriage suddenly felt empty and cold.

Costain had a word with his groom, and the carriage lurched forward at a stately pace. From the window Cathy watched him and Burack hastening along the street, their heads close in discussion, their stride long and purposeful. The groom had apparently been ordered to proceed a little beyond Leonard's house. He drew into the shade of a towering oak, and Cathy lowered the window to look back as Costain and Burack mounted the stairs two at a time and lifted the knocker.

Such an ordinary sight. One might see it any day of the week, two gentlemen calling on a friend, but tonight it filled her with terror. When the door opened and they disappeared inside, she felt as if she would never see them again.

Inside the house, Costain removed his hat and handed it to the aging butler. He retained his cape, as it concealed the bulge of his pistol beneath his jacket. There would be no problem handling the butler. He was scarcely able to walk. "Lord Costain to see Mr. Leonard," he said in an arrogant tone.

"I'm afraid Mr. Leonard is indisposed this evening, milord. If you would care to leave a message . . ."

Costain stared down his aristocratic nose and used a tone Burack had not heard before. "The message, my good man, is that I must see him at once, indisposed or not." He turned aside to Burack and said in an annoyed way, "I daresay this means we must crowd the whole meeting into his bedchamber."

The butler bit his lips and said uncertainly, "Is it—official business, then, your lordship?"

"You don't suppose I am missing the premier ball of the winter for the pleasure of calling on your master?"

The butler was cowed at this show of noble bad manners and said, "If you would care to wait in the saloon, gentlemen, I shall inform Mr. Leonard."

"Be quick about it," Costain said, and looked toward the saloon. The tall, paneled door was closed. A scrabbling sound was suddenly heard on its far side.

"That would be the mistress's dog," the butler said. He walked across the hall and opened the door. Before he could nab it, a tawny pug dog darted out and began leaping at the callers' legs.

Burack directed a malign stare at the animal.

The butler gathered it up in his arms and directed the gentlemen into the saloon. Costain's sharp eyes examined the hallway as he went. There had been water drops on the floor of the entrance hall when they entered, which suggested a recent caller, but there was no sign of Gordon's cape or hat or gloves.

Burack watched to see where the butler went. He first opened a door at the near end of the hall, but he just set the dog down and closed the door again before proceeding down the hallway. He stopped halfway down, tapped at a door on the left side, and entered.

Costain went on ahead into the saloon. It was a small room, but charmingly gotten up in shades of peach and green. With its embossed plaster panels and a graceful white marble fireplace, it seemed a suitable setting for Helena Leonard. A few new pieces of furniture stood out against the faded elegance of an Oriental carpet and slightly fatigued window curtains. It looked like a room in the process of being refurbished—and that suggested more funds than Mr. Leonard could provide by honest means.

In thirty seconds the butler was back. "Mr. Leonard is not in his study. I cannot imagine . . ."

"If he is ill, surely his bedchamber is the place to look," Costain said in a bored drawl.

"Yes, your lordship."

The dog set up a racket behind the closed door when the butler passed. As soon as the butler was beyond hearing, Burack said, "I'm going to have a look in that study."

"Do it quickly, then."

Burack darted down the hall to the study. There was a fire in the grate, and, of more interest, a glass half full of sherry on the corner of the desk. He looked around the room, and noticed the other glass on the carpet, with a dark spot beside it. So two men had been there. Gordon had either been fed doctored sherry, or caught unawares and knocked on the head.

He fled back to the saloon and reported his findings, finishing with the question, "What has he done with the body?"

"Let us hope it is a living, breathing body, and not a corpse. Gordon's been spying on the house. Leonard must have spotted him. It was still a demmed rash thing to abduct the boy. I fear Leonard is way out of his depth. No telling what he might do if we rattle him. I wish we could look around without exciting his suspicions."

"There don't seem to be anyone but the old butler around."

"And a servant or two belowstairs, no doubt. He can't have taken Gordon far. He's in this house somewhere, probably on this floor. He wouldn't want the maids to see him. I assume the whole house is not in on his doings. Why take him upstairs, only to have to bring him down again to—dispose of him."

Death was no new thing to a veteran of the Peninsular War, but this was different. Soldiers took their chances when they enlisted. Gordon was an innocent young civilian. Costain knew he was partly responsible for Gordon's predicament. He had egged the boy on, never imagining such danger awaited him. On top of his guilt, there was the knowledge that he was Cathy's brother. She would despise him if anything happened to Gordon.

He felt fairly sure that the boy had only been drugged. The spilt sherry suggested it. Leonard had panicked. He would want time to assess the situation. Surely murder was not his first option. But it might well be his last. How could he release Gordon after this? They had to find him before Leonard was catapulted by fear into murder.

Costain turned to Burack and spoke in a low, urgent voice. "When the butler comes, you go upstairs and explain the sudden meeting to Leonard.

I'll stay here and ask the butler for tea, to be rid of him, and allow me to search the rooms."

"Very well."

"And Burack—tell Leonard that Cosgrave is awaiting our return, to discover whether Leonard is well enough to take part in this meeting. Just to be sure we do return. You understand?"

"An excellent ploy."

"Only if he believes you. Make the story outrageous enough and he'll be too shocked to consider whether it is true."

Burack grinned. "I'll tell him Boney's been killed and we are going to discuss our options vis-à-vis the war."

"Excellent!"

They heard the echo of approaching feet, and looked up to see not the butler, but Mr. Leonard approaching. They exchanged a defeated look. All their plans were for nought. Again Costain had no one to blame but himself. He had been certain Leonard would stay in bed to bolster his claim of illness. He never thought he would come limping downstairs to meet them.

Leonard wore a dressing gown and leaned on a cane. But Costain knew he had been running down the street, presumably without the aid of his cane, a short while before.

Mr. Leonard said, "What has happened, Lord Costain? Why have you gotten me out of bed at this hour of the night? My butler tells me it is urgent."

Before Costain could reply, Burack blurted out, "Boney is dead. We are all meeting here to discuss it."

Mr. Leonard swallowed it holus-bolus. "Good God, Bonaparte dead! How did it happen?"

Burack looked to Costain. "Fell off his horse and broke his neck," Costain said tersely. "That is all we know yet. Perhaps Castlereagh will have more details when he arrives. We are to search the house—just a precaution—and see that the servants

168

are locked in their rooms. This is too important to risk eavesdroppers. Who is here besides your butler?"

"Just cook and a maid, belowstairs. They will not bother us. I've sent my butler to bed. You have seen how ancient he is." He paused and asked suspiciously, "But why are they meeting here?"

"Because you were not well enough to go to Whitehall, and naturally such discussions would not proceed without you," Costain replied.

"Rubbish! This will be a matter for Liverpool and the Cabinet to thrash out. I cannot believe my presence is that vital," Leonard said. "Meeting in a private house—I never heard of such a thing."

Costain noticed Leonard's hand sliding to the pocket of his dressing gown. His own hand automatically moved under his cape to grip the handle of his pistol, to be ready when Leonard brought out his weapon.

A dead silence fell as the men stared at each other. Without another word being spoken, their own private war was declared, and Costain knew it would be a fight to the death.

Chapter Eighteen

Every minute in the carriage seemed an hour as
Cathy stared at the closed door on Half Moon
Street. What was happening? She was filled with a
dreadful apprehension that not only Gordon but
also Costain and Burack already lay dead on the
floor—although she had heard no sound of gunshots. By the dim light of the moon, she read the
face of her watch once more. It seemed incredible
that only five minutes had passed. Surely the watch
had stopped. But when she held it to her ear, its
steady tick-tick assured her it was working.

She returned her gaze to the door of the Leonard
house. Every square inch of it was etched indelibly
on her memory: the four panels sunk into the solid
oak, two long rectangles below, two shorter ones
above. The door knocker was in the shape of a lion's
head, with a ring suspended from its mouth. The
fanlight above the door had six panes of glass,
rounded at the wide end, to form half a daisy.

How long had it been now? Again she checked
her watch. Six minutes. A quarter of an hour was
too long to wait. She should go and fetch Castlereagh now—except that she could not bring herself

to leave Half Moon Street. What should she do if she heard gunshots? She could hardly leave then. . . .

She heard the clatter of a carriage on the street behind her and turned, hoping against hope that it would be Lord Castlereagh. The side panel did not have a noble crest, but the carriage was indeed drawing to a stop in front of Leonard's house. The footman hopped down and opened the door. Cathy stared to see who got out. It was Mrs. Leonard, alone. She darted into her house without waiting for the butler to open the door. Mrs. Leonard had not become bored with the party and left early; she had not come home to change a slipper that pinched, or a gown that had received a stain. Her hasty movements betrayed a sense of the greatest urgency.

The urgency communicated itself to Cathy as she sat in a fever of indecision. She was about to pull the check string to summon the groom, when a lurch of the carriage told her the groom was descending from his perch. Thirty seconds later his swarthy face appeared at the window.

He opened the door and said, "I'll be taking you back to the ball now, miss. His lordship told me if anyone entered the house—anyone—I was to take you to safety and return."

Cathy was already half up from the seat. "Don't be foolish! We must do something, now."

"I did hate to leave," the groom admitted, "but his lordship is a tiger when he's disobeyed."

She ignored his objection. "Can you peek through the window? The curtains have not been drawn."

"That I can. But you're not to leave the carriage, mind." A dark smile moved his lips as he turned and fled across the street. It had been a long time since he had seen any excitement.

Cathy, watching, could not be certain, but it looked like a pistol he drew from beneath his coat. He disappeared behind a stand of ornamental yews.

An instant later, a head was limned against the lighted window. Whatever he had seen, it propelled him into action. He darted back to the carriage.

"I have to go in there," he said. "I daren't leave, but it's as much as my life is worth to abandon you."

She was out of the carriage even as he spoke. "I'm going with you," she said firmly.

"No, miss. That you are not."

She began running across the street. "Come on," she urged. With a shake of his head, the groom ran after her.

Lord Costain's hand froze in position at the sound of the opening door. As the knocker had not been used, it had to be either Mrs. Leonard returning, or his groom had disobeyed orders. He did not think John Groom would be so rash. Even before Mrs. Leonard appeared, the soft click of a lady's heeled slipper told him who had come. Costain felt little concern at the arrival of a mere lady, except that she added an unnecessary nuisance to the proceedings.

But when he assessed Helena's steely gaze, he felt instinctively he had underestimated this particular lady. She smiled politely, but her flickering gaze had not missed the position of his hand. The dog set up a constant yapping from behind its closed door.

"My dear," Mrs. Leonard said, turning to her husband, "do tell me what is going on. Why are you out of your bed?"

Mr. Leonard's audible sigh of relief was enough to tell Costain who was in charge of matters at Half Moon Street.

"Lord Costain had just told me the most incredible thing," he replied. "It seems—"

"What I told you was in the strictest confidence, Mr. Leonard," Costain said sharply.

Leonard frowned. "Yes, well, as Castlereagh has

172

chosen to use my house, there is no point hoping to keep the meeting secret from my own wife, is there?"

"Meeting?" Mrs. Leonard asked suspiciously. "What meeting?"

"Castlereagh, Cosgrave, myself, and I don't know who else. There has been a great and unexpected occurrence, my dear. Boney is dead! They will all be here in minutes to discuss it."

"Rubbish! Castlereagh and Cosgrave were on their way to supper when I left. There is no meeting. What exactly are you up to, Lord Costain?"

Costain felt the lady's dark eyes assessing him. They held his gaze as if by some demonic force. The fat was in the fire now. He noticed, too, that Leonard told his wife everything. So much for secrecy. She knew this was a hoax, however. His best bet was to move quickly and get the upper hand. As he reached for his pistol, his eyes flickered to Mr. Leonard, to see that he was not drawing his gun. Leonard was looking uncertainly at his wife. Costain quickly whipped out his pistol, and as quickly, a loud crack rent the stillness of the room. His pistol was shot from his hand. He felt a sharp sting, and glancing down, he saw a trickle of blood on his trigger finger. His pistol was on the floor. Mrs. Leonard's smoking gun was aimed at his heart. In the split second that he had averted his eyes from her, she had drawn and aimed at him. Mr. Leonard's gun was also in the open now. And through it all, the dog kept up a constant yapping.

"My dear! Was that necessary?" Harold exclaimed weakly.

"Get their guns, Harold," she ordered in a voice accustomed to command. Harold trotted forward, holding his pistol, and picked Costain's gun up from the floor. He put it in his pocket. Burack handed his over without a word.

"What have you told them?" Mrs. Leonard asked her husband.

"Nothing, my dear. They know nothing."

The glance she threw her husband was full of contempt. "They wouldn't be here if they knew nothing. I told you that boy was watching the house and following me."

After one quick glance at Harold, her eyes remained fixed on Costain and Burack. Costain figured she realized the danger of facing down two husky young men, if her husband did not. He was in no doubt now as to her resolution. She'd shoot them as quickly as she'd powder her nose. His only hope was to negotiate their lives and Gordon's release in return for the Leonards being allowed to escape—for the time being.

"You are quite right," Costain said. "We know everything. You and your house have been watched for some time now."

Her lips curled cynically. "Watch what you say, milord. If I have nothing to lose, then I shan't hesitate to kill you."

"We might yet come to terms," he tempted her. "We are not eager for a scandal at the House Guards. Mr. Leonard will have to retire, of course."

"That might be best, my dear," Leonard said eagerly.

"Retire to raise chickens in the country? I'd rather be dead than buried alive."

"Go to France, then," Burack said angrily. "You should be welcome there, traitor."

Mrs. Leonard sneered. "On the floor, facedown, both of you. I cannot think with all this chatter." To her husband she added, "Tie them up, Harold. Costain first. Don't try anything, Burack, or your friend will pay the price." Her pistol never waivered; it remained steadfastly aimed at Lord Costain while he and Burack reluctantly sank to the floor.

"Ropes," Leonard said.

"Use the belt of your dressing gown."

He put his pistol in his pocket, pulled the sash from his dressing gown, and went nervously toward

Costain, who exchanged a frustrated look with Burack. *I dare not attack Leonard, or she'll kill you,* Burack's look said.

As Leonard leaned over, the hem of his dressing gown trailed the floor. Beneath it, a blue knitted slipper protruded. Costain's arm reached out surreptitiously; his hand gripped Leonard's ankle and he gave a fast, hard yank.

"What the—" Mr. Leonard fell over on top of Burack. Burack quickly rifled the dressing gown pocket, looking in vain for the pistol. Perhaps the gown had two pockets . . .

"Get up, Harold," Helena ordered sharply.

"I fear my shoulder—" He struggled to rise, stumbled. "I must have tripped on my belt," he said in confusion.

When he was standing, Burack rose behind him.

"Back on the floor, Burack," Mrs. Leonard ordered. "Don't think you can use that old fool for a shield. I'll kill him, too, and lay the whole mess in his dish. He is the one who brought me the secrets, after all."

"Ah, Helena, has it come to this?" Mr. Leonard said on a disillusioned sigh. "No longer even the pretence of caring for me, after I have given everything up for you, even my honor?"

"There is no honor among thieves, Harold."

Behind the closed door the dog barked ineffectually as her gun moved slowly from Costain to her husband. Her intention was written on her conniving face. Costain knew she was going to shoot the lot of them. She would claim that Leonard shot Burack and him, then shot himself, as he could not face the shame of his deeds. Her finger began to move on the trigger.

Costain's reaction was instinctive. He lurched toward her. Helena pulled the trigger, and the room reverberated with echoes. He watched in confusion as Helena staggered forward, a wet stain blossoming on the bodice of her burgundy gown. In the ensuing confusion, he thought she had shot herself.

The door from the hallway flew open, and his groom bolted in. Behind him he saw Cathy's pale face, staring in horror at Helena as she sank to the floor. When he looked back, Mr. Leonard had fallen face-forward at his wife's feet.

It was Burack who first grasped the situation. "She shot him! The fiend shot her own husband," he exclaimed.

As they looked at the bodies, Costain noticed the pistol in Leonard's hand. "And he shot her," he said grimly.

Leonard's eyes fluttered open, and Costain rushed to see if he could help him. "Don't blame Helena," Leonard whispered disjointedly. "She meant no harm. She—likes pretty things, and I wanted—to give them to her."

"Burack, send for a sawbones," Costain said.

"No!" Mr. Leonard whispered, clutching Costain's hand. "Let me die in peace—not on the gallows like the traitor I am." His strength was fading. "Tell Lord—Cosgrave I am—sorry."

Costain inclined his head to Leonard's. "Who did you pass the information to? You must tell me, Harold."

"Helena usually—handled that. A milliner—Dutroit—is the messenger—Bond Street." He turned his head and saw Helena's slipper beneath his head. "I die as I lived—at her feet." His eyes rolled up. He died with an ironic smile on his lips.

A momentary hush descended on the room. Even the dog had stopped howling. Into the sudden silence Cathy said, "Where is Gordon? They have not shot him!" Then the dog barked again.

"I wish someone would silence that demmed dog!" Burack said, but no one paid him any heed.

Costain sent his groom off for Lord Castlereagh. Burack went to the dining room and found a sealed bottle of sherry. He prepared a tray and brought it to the living room. While he poured, Costain went to the two bodies on the floor and moved Mr. Leonard so that he lay side by side with his wife, then he took a seat on the couch beside Cathy.

"Why did you do that?" she asked.

He took her fingers and squeezed them very hard. "Now that he's dead, he is no longer at her feet."

"Was she the spy?"

"She seduced him into doing the spying for her. I wager that is why she married him. I shouldn't be surprised if she put Fotherington up to the same thing at Amiens. She is the one who trotted the secrets to the Frenchies, as Gordon thought."

"About Gordon, Costain—"

He set down his glass. "Yes, we must find him. We think he is on this floor. Burack—"

"Let me put that demmed dog out before we do anything else," Burack said. He went to the room off the hall and opened the door. The dog did not leap at him as he expected. Instead, it trotted behind a sofa and resumed its barking.

When Burack went to investigate, he found Gordon's inert body on the floor, a cushion beneath his head. Poor old Harold; he was not cut out for this work. He was too soft by half. Burack leaned over Gordon, felt his heart, and was confident that he would soon sleep off the laudanum.

He called Cathy, and with Costain's help got Gordon onto the sofa. "It will be best if we just close this door and say nothing about your being here," Costain said to Cathy. "I shall return for you later."

"Mama will be looking for me."

"I'll send word to her that you were feeling unwell and I took you home."

Burack took the dog by the scruff of the neck, carried it down to the kitchen, and closed the door.

Chapter Nineteen

There was considerable confusion in the house on Half Moon Street that night. Mysterious unmarked carriages arrived, and gentlemen darted into the house, their hats pulled low over their eyes to conceal their faces. Eventually two large objects were removed from the house under heavy wraps.

Castlereagh was the first to arrive. When he had been put in possession of the major facts—Costain did not consider it crucial to inform his superior that the Lymans were even then in the room across the hall—he settled down with a bottle of port to devise a story that would minimize speculation and scandal. It was Costain who came up with the idea that the Leonards had engaged in a tragic lovers' quarrel, ending in a suicide-murder.

"It might just do," Castlereagh said with a weary smile. "Helena Leonard was enough to drive a man to murder. Cosgrave had no idea what she was up to, of course, but it is the end of his career. He never could keep his hands off a pretty woman. When I asked him if she was his mistress, he denied it, of course. We cannot have that sort of carry-on in our top lads. I shall suggest a quiet retirement, to save his face. He has rendered good service in the past. No need to publicly humiliate the fellow, but I shall ring a peal over him behind closed doors." He cast a speculative glance at Costain. "That leaves me with the problem of finding a replacement for Cosgrave."

"I suggest you use Cosgrave's deficiencies as a bat to beat York and his cronies over the head and appoint your own man," Costain said.

"My thinking exactly. I should prefer a younger gentleman. There's no fool like an old fool, when all's said and done."

Costain ignored that speculative look. "As the Leonards' demise was a matter of simple homicide, we ought to call in Bow Street," he said.

"Yes, by God. We'll let Townsend handle the disposal of the bodies in the usual way. I shall tip him the clue that he must handle the nominal investigation personally." He turned to an aide and asked him to send for the top Bow Street officer.

They then discussed means of rounding up the other members of the gang until Townsend arrived and had a brief talk with Castlereagh. Townsend arranged the removal of the bodies.

After he left, Costain said, "A Mademoiselle Dutroit, a Bond Street milliner, is involved, and probably a modiste, Madame Marchand. You might want to watch their shops for the next few days. I expect they are only go-betweens."

"I see you have been busy!" Castlereagh said approvingly.

"I had help. Young Lyman has been doing some legwork for me. An excellent chap, and not so hotheaded as you feared. He is interested in a position at the Horse Guards, by the bye."

"I'll speak to him. As I said, we need younger men." He set down his glass and rose. "I think that is about it for this evening. A fine job, Costain. Are you returning to the ball?"

"I shall remain here awhile, to have a look

179

around the house. Burack tells me there are some documents in Leonard's office."

Castlereagh turned to Burack. "Would you mind taking them down to the Horse Guards tonight? Such things should never leave the premises. Cosgrave!" He shook his head.

Burack went to gather up the documents, and Castlereagh said to Costain, "Drop by my office tomorrow morning and we shall discuss Cosgrave's replacement. Are you interested in the job yourself? I know you planned to return to Spain. Anyone with good eyesight and a steady hand can aim a gun."

"There is a little more to it than that, milord."

"Of course there is. I did not mean to disparage our excellent soldiers. My meaning is that you would be of more use here. Think about it, lad." He patted Costain's shoulder and left.

Burack came hurrying out of the study and rushed after Castlereagh, to enlarge upon his own part in the evening, and hint for an increase in salary.

As soon as he was gone, Costain darted into the room across the hall. Cathy sat in the light of one flickering candle, Gordon's head in her lap. She looked tired and frightened. He wanted to take her into his arms. He hurried to her side and just patted her shoulder. "Are you all right?" he asked.

She smiled trustingly. "Thank you for keeping us out of it, Costain. I daresay we would have had to appear in court and all sorts of unpleasant things if Castlereagh had known we were here. Has he left?"

"For the moment, but Townsend will be returning."

"Gordon is coming to now, but he is very confused. I should like to take him home. He ought to be in bed."

"I'll ask my groom to help get him to the carriage."

While this was going forth, the dog reappeared, sniffing about the floor and whining piteously. Gordon opened his eyes. "Oh, Lord, not that curst mutt again!" he said, then closed his eyes again.

"Perhaps May senses that something untoward has happened to her mistress," Cathy said, gazing sadly at the dog. "Poor little thing. Who will look after her?" The dog came and sat at her ankles, gazing at her with moist brown eyes. Cathy lifted her up and stroked her. "We cannot leave her here alone."

"She is not alone," Costain said. "There are servants in the house."

"I wish I could take her home, but Mama would have a fit."

"I'll take her," Costain said, and put the dog under his arm, where it yelped its gratitude. In the carriage it settled peacefully at Costain's feet.

Gordon revived during the drive home and insisted on Costain's coming in to hear his story, and to relate all that had happened while he was unconscious. John Groom was given the job of watching the dog. Cathy ordered coffee and sandwiches, and they ate ravenously while Costain explained the night's proceedings.

It was this homey sight that greeted Lady Lyman's eyes when she returned from the ball. The three of them looked as guilty as sinners when she entered. What was going on here? "I made sure you would be in bed, Cathy," she exclaimed. "Did you not have a fit of megrims at the ball?"

"I am feeling better now, Mama."

"We all decided that what ailed us was hunger, so we had some sandwiches and coffee made," Gordon said. "Don't let us keep you, Mama. You look burnt to the socket."

"I am not used to these late nights. You look peaked yourself, Gordon. Don't stay up too late."

Gordon wondered why Costain accompanied Lady Lyman to the staircase and stayed a full five minutes talking to her. For her part, Lady Lyman could scarcely believe her luck. An invitation to Northland Abbey for the whole family for Christmas! It could be no less than a formal betrothal Costain had in mind. Rag-mannered of him to have stayed so late—it was two-thirty! Odd, too, that Cathy was still up and about when she had retired from the ball with a headache. Lady Lyman was pretty sure Gordon had been drunk. He looked exceedingly pale. The bandage Costain was wearing on his hand suggested he had been in some sort of brawl. Perhaps Costain had beaten up Burack for having taken Cathy out. Such a hotheaded husband would be a handful for Cathy to manage, but he would soon be rushing back to Spain, so that would be all right.

In the saloon, Gordon said to his sister, "Costain is bamming Mama with some story to turn her up sweet."

When Costain returned to the saloon, Gordon said, "Did you tell Castlereagh about my part in all this?"

"I could not think you wanted him to know you had been overpowered by Leonard," Costain explained. "As to the rest, he is aware of your involvement. It was you who put us on to Dutroit and Marchand. It will take a few days to round up all their cohorts."

"What about Cosgrave? He was certainly making up to Mrs. Leonard."

"Indeed he was, but that is all he was doing. He'll be dismissed, of course, but no charges will be laid. Helena used her liaison with Cosgrave to gain her husband a position at the Horse Guards—for what purpose you may imagine. We will never know for certain now, but I imagine she convinced Harold that she would leave him if he could not provide more of the niceties of life. He could not do it honestly; no doubt she suggested how he could do it dishonestly."

Gordon nodded. "If I had caught a glimpse of his stubby fingers sooner, I could have solved the case in a minute. I think you were wrong to keep me away from the office, Costain. I knew as soon as he handed me the sherry that he was our man. What I did not think was that he would recognize me in a shot, from breaking into our office here."

"Mrs. Leonard had spotted you lurking about the house, too," Costain said. "You must be more careful another time."

"It won't happen again. I wonder what brought her rushing home before the ball was half over."

"There was a note in her purse from Harold, telling her that he had you under sedation at the house, asking what he should do. I daresay she saw Burack and Cathy and myself rushing away from the ball, and decided she'd best get home to take charge."

"How does it come you never suspected Mr. Leonard, Costain?" Cathy asked.

"I thought he was too timid to tackle such a daring thing. I am certain he hated every minute of it. He was a pattern-card of conscientiousness at work, always hounding everyone to follow the rules. And to discover at the end that his wife despised him." He shook his head and gave a quiet *tsk*. "At least he never learned she was carrying on with Cosgrave."

"About my joining the staff at the Horse Guards, Costain," Gordon said. "You mentioned something about another time. With Leonard gone, they'll need a replacement. Who do you think will take Cosgrave's spot? I'll see if Mama knows him, and can put in a word for me."

Costain cleared his throat modestly. "Actually, Castlereagh has suggested that I take over from Cosgrave."

Gordon's exclamations of delight went unheard by Cathy. She was looking at Costain with a smile trembling on her lips. "Then you would not be returning to Spain?" she asked.

"He has half convinced me I could be of more use here."

"Only half?" Gordon asked in astonishment. "Why, it would be great fun, Costain. You and me and Burack—what a team!"

"I am giving the matter my serious consideration. There are a few points to clarify first."

"What does it hinge on?" Gordon asked at once.

Costain's dark eyes turned to Cathy. "On a lady," he said.

Gordon's youthful visage assumed a sneer. "You are ill-advised to chart your course on the whim of a lady. I daresay Miss Stanfield never even noticed I was missing."

"On the contrary, she was very much put out by your cavalier treatment at the ball. You must apologize nicely when you meet her at Northland at Christmas."

"Eh? What the devil are you talking about? I shall not be—I say, are you inviting me to Northland?"

"Your mama was kind enough to accept an invitation on behalf of the family." He gazed at Cathy, watching the light flush that bloomed in her cheeks and the shy smile that lit her eyes.

"And Miss Stanfield is going, you say?" Gordon said.

Costain cast an impatient glance at this nuisance of a boy. "How else can I hope to gain a few moments privacy with your sister?" he replied with a meaningful look.

"Good Lord! You don't mean Cathy is the lady you were talking about?"

"Perhaps if you wrote Miss Stanfield a nice note of apology, Gordon—*now*," Costain suggested.

"By Jove, I'll do it first thing in the morning."

"Never leave till tomorrow what can be done today," Costain urged.

184

"It *is* tomorrow. I mean to say, it's after two. I can hardly deliver a note at three o'clock in the morning."

"You could write it."

"Yes, but—"

Costain rose and took Gordon by the elbow to usher him from the room. "Good night, Gordon. Remember who is now in charge of hiring at the Horse Guards."

"She hasn't said yes, Costain." On that parting shot, Gordon finally strode from the room.

Costain returned and took up the seat beside Cathy on the sofa. "Between dogs and brothers and mamas, it is hard to find a moment's privacy."

"Will you keep the dog?" Cathy asked, though she did not really care much at that point.

"That, too, depends on a lady's answer," he said, taking her hand and stroking it. "I am not above bribery, you see. A thoroughly bad article."

"I think you are very nice."

"Nice? *Nice!* Good God, what have I done to deserve such lukewarm praise?"

"And brave," she added.

His arm moved around her shoulder and tugged her closer. "That is better. Pray, continue."

"Well, you are a baron."

"Run dry so soon, have we? To praise a man's title suggests he is no better than a turnip. The best part of him is buried. I am also trustworthy."

"You should not have brought that letter to me for translation."

"Let us call it independent. Also honest." He flicked a curl that hung loose at her temple.

"You lied about that letter, and the suicide-murder."

He gave a little yank at her curl. "We call that inventive. My poaching on Burack's date is harder to whitewash."

"Seizing an opportunity?" she suggested helpfully.

"Wide awake on all suits. My practicing nepotism on Gordon's behalf I shall call family loyalty. And speaking of family—" He drew her into his arms.

Her eyes were wide and bright with anticipation. "Yes, Costain?" she asked in a breathless voice.

"I am flattered at your eagerness, but I haven't asked you yet!"

"We cannot ascribe undue haste to you, in any case."

His smile firmed to sincerity. When he spoke, the bantering tone had changed to something akin to shyness. "Nor even much courage, in such delicate matters as this, but whatever my faults, I love you very much. I shall make you a good husband, Cathy, if you'll have me. Will you?"

She gazed a moment at this handsome, dashing lord, hardly able to believe that he could love her, but his glowing eyes assured her that he did. "Yes, I will," she said simply, and was pulled ruthlessly into his arms for a kiss that left her giddy. His hands stroked her back, and moved down to span her waist, crushing her against his chest while his lips firmed to passion.

She knew her life had changed irrevocably. No more sitting in the study, waiting for the occasional tap at the door. No more vicarious romance from gothic novels and translating other people's billets-doux. No dull Christmas, listening to Mama's memories of the good times long past. Now it was her turn to live. The Great Winter Ball had performed its magic after all, even if she had not attended with Costain.

She reluctantly drew back and gazed at him, smiling fatuously. "Just think, if you had not come to me with that letter, or if Uncle Rodney had been there, or if Mr. Leonard had not come, forcing me to run after you . . ."

"But I did, and Uncle Rodney wasn't, and Mr. Leonard did. It must be fate." There was a sound of footsteps in the hallway. "That doesn't sound like fate, however. More like Gordon."

Gordon peered in. "I say, Costain, would you mind having a look at this note for Miss Stanfield? P'raps we'd best go into the study. You go and tell Mama your news, Cathy. She won't be able to believe it. Oh, congratulations and all that, Costain. I see by her witless grin that she accepted. Now, about this letter, do you think *My Dear Miss Stanfield* or just *Dear Miss Stanfield* or—"

Costain's mobile brows rose in impatience, then settled down again. "I shall call on you tomorrow, Cathy. My family loyalty has other duties for me now. *À demain.*"

He escorted her to the foot of the stairs, placed a light kiss on her cheek, and watched as she ascended, with many stops to look behind her.

Gordon took his elbow and ushered him into the study. "You know Miss Stanfield better than I. Do you think I should apologize, or give her a bit of a ragging for standing up with Edison?"

With a last look over his shoulder at his beloved, Costain sighed and turned his attention to the matter at hand.